Me, My Goat, & My Sister's Wedding

Me, My Goat, & My Sister's Wedding

STELLA PEVSNER

Clarion Books
TICKNOR & FIELDS: A HOUGHTON MIFFLIN COMPANY
New York

Clarion Books
Ticknor & Fields, a Houghton Mifflin Company
Copyright © 1985 by Stella Pevsner

Printed in the U.S.A.

Library of Congress Cataloging in Publication Data
Pevsner, Stella.
Me, my goat, and my sister's wedding.

Summary: Doug and his friends keep their pet goat a secret from their
families, but before long, sightings of the high-spirited animal occur at
very inappropriate places.
1. Children's stories, American.   [1. Goats—Fiction]   I. Title.
PZ7.P44815Me 1985   [Fic]   84-12734
ISBN 0-89919-305-6

V   10 9 8 7 6 5 4 3 2 1

Contents

1. More Fun Than a Barrel of Monkeys · 1
2. Just a Simple Garden Ceremony · 12
3. Getting Ready for Rudy · 18
4. Money Troubles Ahead · 25
5. Love at First Sniff · 33
6. A Surprise for Missy · 43
7. It's Just a Joke, Honk-Honk · 52
8. This Goat's a Living Lawnmower · 61
9. Rudy Gets Rainboots · 71
10. Just a Hillbilly Goat · 83
11. Rudy Goes to Work · 95
12. Disaster Down the Street · 108
13. In a Whole Bunch of Trouble · 114
14. Maybe Mom Will Marry Larry · 125
15. Missy Meets April and June · 134
16. Good-bye, Rudy · 146
17. An Uninvited Wedding Guest · 154
18. The Wicked Step-Sisters Take Off · 165
19. And They Lived Happily Ever After · 173

For Barbara E., with thanks

Me, My Goat, & My Sister's Wedding

CHAPTER 1

More Fun Than a Barrel of Monkeys

WHENEVER WOODY GETS excited or embarrassed, his ears turn a fiery red. They were pretty bright-looking the day we had the meeting at the club. He was spitting out little specks as he talked, too. Woody does that when he's excited and also saying something. Sometimes, when he does the spitting number, Frank and I, just to annoy him, pretend we're holding umbrellas in front of our faces.

That June afternoon of the meeting, though, we didn't do anything to upset Woody. He was plenty worked up enough as it was.

"Guys," he said, "this is big stuff I'm bringing before the membership today." Pause. "Big stuff."

"Yeah? Let's hear it." Frank said.

We were what you might call casual at our meetings. Membership was down to just the three of us. We took turns being president for a month at a time.

Woody took a deep breath and then turned to me. "You, Douglas," he said, "as past president, you know how hard it is for kids our age to earn an honest dollar or two."

"I, Frank," Frank butted in, "as another past president, know it too. So is this your big, hot news item that we all came here to the clubhouse to hear about?"

"Not exactly," Woody said with a fatherly smile.

"We're broke," Frank said. "So what else is new?"

"Just this," Woody said. "There is a way. A way to do a friend a favor and make megabucks at the same time."

"So spit it out," Frank said. As a reflex he raised the imaginary umbrella. "I haven't got all day. My tuba lesson's in an hour and a half, and I ought to get in some practice."

"I shall be brief, then," Woody said. "I found out that Oliver Newhart is going on a two-week backpack trip. And you know what Oliver Newhart has."

"Kind of a bad smell," I said.

"True," Woody agreed, "but the important thing is this: Oliver Newhart has a goat. And he needs a goat-sitter for the time he'll be gone."

A light dawned. "You mean," I asked, "he wants us to take care of his goat? For two weeks? For pay?"

"You got the idea," Woody said. "Well, men, what do you think?"

"I think you're nuts," Frank said. "I'm not going to bike way out there where Oliver lives, just to toss garbage or tin cans to some stupid animal."

"But that's just it. We don't need to bike anywhere.

Because the goat would be our guest. Here. In the clubhouse."

"Hey, neat!" I said.

"Here?" Frank looked around. "We just painted the place. The goat would mess it all up."

"With our money from goat-tending, we could hire interior decorators to come in afterward and do the entire . . . well . . . this one room we have . . . in style," Woody said.

"It sure looks like easy money," I said. "Besides, it would be a lot of fun. I've always wanted a goat."

"Yeah, well, it sounds like fun all right," Frank had to admit. "Just so long as we keep the goat right here. My mom would throw some kind of fit if I ever took it home."

"There's no need to take it anyplace," Woody said. "We can make the clubhouse nice and comfortable. And of course, we'll take turns coming down to feed the goat and care for his needs." He smiled. "This place down here, away from the houses, is made to order."

He was right. We live on the outskirts of town. This area used to be on the wild side, with lots of trees and bushes and a little creek running through. The creek's still here, but some of the trees and stuff have been cleared away for new houses.

"What'll your dad say, Doug?" Frank wanted to know. "He kind of owns this clubhouse."

"He does not," I said. "It may be closest to our house, but it belongs to the kids in all the families around here."

"That comes down to just the three of us guys, now

that the Boyd twins have moved away."

"Maybe we should start grooming your brother for membership," Woody said to Frank.

"Are you out of your mind? Austin's only three and a half, and he isn't always dry, if you get what I mean."

"Girls can belong too, you know," I said. "My two big sisters were members when they were kids."

"Girls in the club? That's a really sickening idea," Frank said. He was in a bad mood. Frank was always in a bad mood the day of his tuba lesson.

Woody checked his watch. "Could we get back to today's issue? Oliver will be here any minute. I told him I had to present his idea to the membership before we talked to him. He wanted to come around anyway, to check out this place himself. Just to be sure it's the right thing for Rudy." Rudy it turned out, was the name of Oliver's goat.

Frank looked at his own watch. It had an alarm on it, but Frank didn't know how to set it because the instructions were in Japanese. "I can't stick around much longer," he said. "If I'm late one more time I'll be grounded, Mom says."

"Let's go outside and wait," Woody said. "Oliver might have gotten lost or fallen into the creek. Not that he'd drown or anything. How deep is it? Would you say four or five inches?"

"About."

We wandered outside and looked at the creek. The water was barely moving. "One time the creek was higher. After spring rains," I said, "and the kids built a

4

raft. Only by the time they got it together the creek had gone down. They made it into a bridge instead. That was a long time ago, when my older sister belonged."

"Just how old is she now, anyway?" Frank asked.

"Sylvia? She's real old. About twenty-nine, maybe even thirty. I lost track. Anyway, she's got this kid now who's ten."

"How come we've never met him? The kid?"

"For one thing, it's a *she*. Melissa. Missy, we call her. For another, they live in Minneapolis. They're divorced. From the father, I mean. They come to visit once in a while, but I guess you guys have never been around."

"I'm not going to be around much longer, either, if this Oliver doesn't show up pronto." Frank tossed a pebble into the creek.

Just then we heard a rustle and, turning around, we saw Oliver cutting through bushes down at the bottom of the Parker property.

"Hey, Oliver, over here," Woody yelled. To us, in an undertone, he said, "Now, listen, when he tells us about taking care of the goat, act like it's a lot of hard work. That way he may up the ante. The payment."

It was annoying the way Woody was always using some term and then explaining it as though we were really stupid.

"Hey, Oliver, glad to see you!" Woody said. "You know Doug here. . . ."

"Yeah."

"And this is Frank."

"Hi."

Oliver cocked a thumb toward the clubhouse. "This the place you were telling me about?"

"Sure is," Woody said. "Come inside and have a look."

We all went in. I thought it was looking great with the new orange paint job and all, but Oliver didn't seem impressed. "There's a board loose over there," he said. "It'll make a draft. Rudy's not used to drafts."

"We were about to fix that," I said. "We always do a little fixing up this time of year." That was true. Only last year we nailed a new shingle on the roof because we got tired of rain leaking in on our heads.

"There's no feed bin," Oliver observed. "Rudy won't eat off the floor."

"Heck, we could easily build a bin," I said. "Couldn't we, guys?"

"Sure," Frank said.

"Frank is a handy man with a hammer," Woody added.

Oliver checked the door. "I see hinges here, but where's the padlock? You might not think that people would kidnap a goat, but stranger things happen every day. Just read the papers."

"The old padlock rusted out this last winter," I said. "We had to file it off. But we'll get a new one for sure."

"Better make it a combination kind. There are too many people around who can pick locks. Read the papers."

6

Boy, I'd never known this Oliver kid was so paranoid. He took his time looking around, then walked outside and checked the clubhouse from all sides. "Any of you guys have a dog?"

Both Frank and I told him yes. Then I asked why.

"Goats get lonesome. They want some kind of companion. So one of you would have to leave your dog here with Rudy all night and sometimes during the day."

"You know my dog, Prince," I said to the guys. "He'd love Rudy." The fact was that Prince loved everyone. He might be a little short on brains, but he sure was friendly.

Oliver, frowning, walked the few yards down to the creek and looked up and down. Then he walked away from us, still looking around.

"What's he doing?" I said in an undertone. "What's his problem?"

"Don't you see?" Woody murmured back. "He's trying to psych us out, making it look like some big deal."

"Well, it is a big decision," Frank said. "Leaving his goat somewhere. If I owned a pet like that, I'd be careful, too. About who I left it with, I mean."

"Yeah, well just act casual," Woody advised. "Don't let him make you nervous. That would give him the upper hand." He stepped forward to meet Oliver, who was coming back. "So? What do you think?" he asked. "Like the looks of our layout?"

"It's not bad," Oliver said, unwrapping a stick of

gum and jamming it into his mouth. "Provided you come up with some improvements. I'll keep you guys in mind."

In mind! I could see Rudy slipping out of our grasp. And just when I'd been thinking what a great time we'd have, messing around with a real live goat. "You mean we've got competition? There are some other places where Rudy might stay?"

"Naturally." Oliver stuck his thumbs in his jeans pockets and stood there looking at us as though he was some hotshot cowhand. "As I said before, Rudy means too much to me — to our whole family — to just leave him anywhere. I've got to make sure he gets grade-A attention."

"Hey, we'd take super care of him!" Frank was all but jumping up and down. "I swear we would, wouldn't we, guys?"

"We sure would."

"Well, then," Oliver said, "since I have your ironclad promise, I might just go along with you. I'll even sell you fodder for him, at a good discount. That's because I really believe you'll do the best by Rudy." He shifted the wad of gum. "As for the fee . . ."

"Fee? What fee?" Woody asked in a weak sort of voice.

"*What fee?*" Oliver looked as though he just couldn't believe the question. "Why, the entertainment fee. What do you think?" And then as we all stood silently, our mouths more or less hanging open, Oliver went on, "A goat like Rudy is more fun than a barrel of monkeys. Why, you won't have to go to the movies, the game arcades, anywhere. You'll have too much fun hanging around that goat."

I gave my head a little shake as though to clear my brain. What was going on here, anyway? Woody and Frank looked just as confused.

"You mean," Woody finally managed to stammer, "you want *us* to pay *you*?"

"It wouldn't be much," Oliver said, "since we're friends. I'd say . . . oh . . . five dollars a week."

"Each?" Frank yelped.

Woody jabbed him with an elbow. "What makes you think we should pay?" He gave Oliver a stern look. "You're talking a lot of work. A lot of responsibility."

"And a lot of fun," Oliver reminded. "A whole barrel of fun."

He had us there. I was itching for the chance to play with Rudy for two whole weeks. "We don't have five dollars," I said carefully. "In fact, the club treasury is down to about thirty cents."

Oliver didn't look concerned. "So? What's wrong with bankrolling it from your allowances?"

Woody cleared his throat. "Just a moment, Oliver. I need to confer with the membership."

We walked off a short distance. "What do you think, guys?" he whispered.

"You said we were going to *make* money," Frank said. "Not pay it out."

"Yeah, but Oliver's right," I said. "About it being fun. I've always wanted a goat."

"And what are our allowances for, if not to spend as we like?" Woody said. "What do you say, fellas. Should we go for it?"

"All right," Frank agreed. "But make him lower the price. I'm not all that flush."

We walked back to Oliver. "We're prepared to offer you three dollars a week," Woody said.

"Four."

"Three and a half."

Oliver looked hurt. Then he shrugged and said, "Well, what is money when you're dealing with friends. Right? So okay. Three and a half."

As we were shaking hands all around, a sudden blast of a bugle broke the quiet.

Frank jumped. "That's Mom! And you know what that means!" He took off at a run.

"Frank's mom blows that bugle," I told Oliver, "as a last resort when she's called and called and he doesn't answer."

"I've got to get going, too," Oliver said. "So, guys, be thinking of how you're going to get Rudy over here." He paused and then shrugged. "Oh, shoot. I'll get my dad to haul him over in the truck. No extra fee. You sure caught me in a good-natured mood today. So long." He took off along the creek bank.

As Woody and I stood there alone, I glanced at him and then away. He looked embarrassed and for once seemed to be at a loss for words.

I kicked at a chunk of dirt. "Hey, Woody. We can make money for the club some other way. There's no rule that says we can't entertain ourselves. And anyway, it's no big deal. Seven dollars for the two weeks, split three ways . . ."

"We'd better not count on Frank," Woody said, still looking uneasy. "As you know, any little thing he does wrong, his mother cuts off his allowance."

"Yeah. But if just you and I kick in, it still comes to only three fifty apiece."

Woody gave a sigh of relief and put a hand on my shoulder. "You're a good man, Doug. As club president, I've come to rely on your support and you have never let me down."

"That's okay," I mumbled. We shook hands and parted.

At that time he'd probably forgotten about the extra cost of the feed. I know I had.

Walking up the incline toward our house, it suddenly came to me that we'd made a heavy-duty decision. We'd agreed to keep that goat for two whole weeks without even checking to see what our parents might have to say. With the other two guys it might not matter so much. They lived quite a distance away. But the clubhouse was just down the incline from our backyard.

How would Mom and Dad react to the idea of having a goat guest so close to the house?

Not well, I thought. *Not well at all*.

CHAPTER 2

Just a Simple Garden Ceremony

A s I dragged my way toward the house I com-
puted the whole situation. By the time I reached
the back door I knew three things:

1. I wanted to have Rudy around. What kid
   wouldn't?
2. My parents wouldn't want to have Rudy
   around. What parents would?
3. Woody, Frank, and I would have to think up
   ways of keeping Rudy under wraps, at least
   at first. After a while, when the goat was
   settled into some sort of routine, he'd be no
   problem. Our parents might even admire the
   way we took care of him.

I opened the screen door and started across the back
porch. Like the back porches in most of the older
houses in the neighborhood, ours is screened in. On

really hot nights I sleep out there on a studio couch. I never do, though, if I've just seen something creepy on TV.

The screen door whamped shut behind me. Mom called out, "Is that you, Doug?"

I made some cackling hen noises and said, "No, it's just us chickens."

Inside, I saw Mom seated at the kitchen counter by the telephone. It seemed to me she was always on the phone these days. If she wasn't calling long distance to see how her sister, my aunt Harriet, was doing, she was calling about wedding plans for Gloria.

My sister was getting married in a couple of weeks. I hadn't mentioned it at the clubhouse meeting because we have a rule that says we have to stick to important issues. The guys probably knew about it anyway. The whole town, it seemed, knew Gloria and Greg were getting married. In fact, the whole state of Illinois probably knew.

"Where have you been, Chicken?" Mom asked me. And then before I could answer, she added, "I'm really worried about Harriet."

"Is she still sick?" I took the carton of orange juice out of the refrigerator. Mom used to buy me soft drinks, but the last time Sylvia and Missy were here, my big sister did a number about all the terrible things soda does to a kid's insides. Mom lets a lot of things Sylvia says influence her.

"Still sick?" Mom repeated. "Oh, Doug, your aunt Harriet's very sick. She may need surgery for those kidney stones."

I put the juice back after I'd poured a glassful. "How come you don't go visit her, like Dad says you should?"

"I don't know." Mom was looking off into space, frowning a little. "I feel I should . . . and yet with Gloria's . . ."

"It's no big deal about the wedding, is it?" I flopped into a chair by the kitchen table. "Just a simple garden ceremony? That's what you said."

"True, but still, there's the cake, flowers, champagne. I shouldn't have let these things go for so long."

Prince woke up from his nap, sniffed, and then came padding over to me. He was on the prowl for food, as usual. "It's only orange juice," I said, and held it down so he could take a sniff. He licked the rim of the glass anyway.

That was another thing that gave my sister Sylvia fits. Prince licking plates and things. I told her it's a well-known fact that dogs' mouths are clean. In fact, a human bite is more lethal than a dog's. Sylvia then said it was a case of good hygiene. She always has to have the last word. I don't see how Missy can stay so calm and good-natured with a mother like that.

At supper that night, no one talked a whole lot. Dad was probably thinking about the editorial he had to write for his weekly paper. Mom was probably thinking about Aunt Harriet. I was thinking about the goat. It was hard, ever, to guess what Gloria was thinking about.

Finally, Dad got that satisfied look that meant he'd come up with some subject that would knock everyone's socks off. Then he turned his attention to Gloria. "How are your wedding plans progressing?" he asked.

"Oh, fine," she told him. "Greg and I have decided to have two."

Wow. Lucky for me, I thought, that my folks didn't stop with just Sylvia and Gloria. "Maybe three kids would be better," I said.

Gloria laughed. "Oh, Doug!" She even blushed a little. I could see why, with that delicate pink complexion, big blue eyes, and soft blond hair, people called her a living doll.

"Honey, I was talking about *rings*." She frowned slightly. "But I guess with my engagement and wedding rings and Greg's matching band, it does make three."

My parents, who long ago had gotten used to Gloria's odd way of thinking, just smiled. Then Mom's worried look returned. "Oh, Clarence, I'm just so worried about Harriet."

"No better?" Dad asked.

"They think she'll have to go in for surgery. I feel, in a way, that I ought to go there to be with her."

"I've been saying all along that you should," Dad said. "She's your only sister, after all. You'll feel a lot better if you go."

"But the wedding. I need to order flowers, cake . . ."

"Now, Alice," Dad said, resting his hand on top of Mom's on the table, "those are only details. Why can't Gloria handle those. Gloria?"

"What?" My sister blinked and smiled.

"I said . . ." My father took a deep breath. "I said,

Why can't you handle the details? You can, can't you?"

"But of course I can!" Gloria's smile suddenly stopped. "What details?"

Dad looked at the ceiling.

"Your dumb wedding," I said.

"Honey," Mom said to my sister, "your father thinks I should go to see how Harriet is doing, and to give her some encouragement. And we're wondering if you could take over some of the plans. For the ceremony."

"The wedding? Sure!" Gloria stopped to consider. "What would I do?"

Mom and Dad exchanged glances. I guess it's hard on them, being bright themselves, to have someone like my sister to raise. At least it wouldn't be for much longer. Provided her boyfriend, Greg, didn't back out. He probably didn't care about Gloria's mind, though. He was so crazy in love with her looks and sweet disposition.

Dad suddenly snapped his fingers. "Sylvia! There's the answer. Sylvia!"

"What about Sylvia?" Mom asked.

"Didn't she say, when she called last week, that she's finished with the new fashion line?"

"Yes. But what . . . ?"

"She's got the time. Missy's out of school. So let Sylvia come here and take charge."

"Oh, Clarence, I'd hate to impose . . ."

"Now, Alice, who was it that took care of Missy when Sylvia went to the West Coast that time? And who nursed Missy through the measles?"

"I love having Missy here, sick or not." Mom got up

to pour coffee. "But you're right, hon. This is a family emergency of sorts. And if Sylvia is willing . . ."

"Call her," Dad said. "Call her tonight. And then call Bill and Harriet. And after that, call about train reservations. Once you've gone there and done whatever needs to be done, your mind will be more at ease."

Great, I thought. *Great for them, but not for me*. Without Mom around to run interference, that Sylvia would mop the floor with me.

There was one consolation, though. Except for when I'd have to be in the house for meals and sleeping, I'd have a good place to get away from my sister's bossiness. I'd hang out in the clubhouse with Rudy. He'd help make time go fast until Mom got back home.

I held out a piece of pot roast for Prince and then let him lick my fingers. *Old buddy, you're in for some bad times*, I thought, *if that Sylvia takes charge around here*. Prince looked at me, his eyes kind of rolling around, as though he could read my mind. I guess, though, he was wondering if I'd hand him another piece of pot roast.

I did.

CHAPTER 3

Getting Ready for Rudy

WOODY CALLED LATER that night. "I've been doing research on goats," he said. "We're going to have to work fast tomorrow, to fix up the place for Rudy."

"Fix it up how?"

"Get rid of any drafts, for one thing. And build the feed bin."

"You really think Frank knows how to build one?"

"Of course. His dad's taught him everything there is to know about carpentry. We can get the wood there, too. I'll stop by for you at about nine."

Mom walked into the kitchen just then and seemed to be waiting for me to hang up. "I've got to go," I told Woody. "See you tomorrow."

"What are you kids up to now?" Mom asked. But she said it in a way that didn't seem to require an answer. She went on, "I'm leaving in the morning, did I tell you? But Sylvia can't get here until Sunday. I'm wondering what you'll do in the meantime."

"What do you mean?"

"I guess you won't starve, though. There are things in the freezer. And plenty of places to eat out, if it comes to that."

"Mom, come on. We're not kids." *Kids. Baby goats.* Everything reminded me of Rudy.

She sat down at the table, and I went over and put my arm around her shoulders. She circled my waist with her arm. "Mom," I said, "you should have let Dad buy you that microwave oven like he wanted to."

"I guess. But it seemed such a useless expense. After all, I'm around here all the time and have plenty of time for cooking."

This was true enough. My mother is the old-fashioned kind, who bakes things from scratch and makes her own gravy. I wished instead of going to visit her sick sister my Mom could take a vacation to Hawaii or St. Louis or somewhere. She deserved it.

"Are you taking the train?"

"Yes. Your father will drive me to the station, and then he'll go directly to the office. You'll be at loose ends all day. I'm sure I can trust you, though."

I felt just the least bit guilty. "Trust me how?"

"Oh . . . not to make a mess in the house. Not to do any of those smelly and dangerous chemistry experiments in your room. Not to . . . get sick from eating all kinds of junk."

"Mom," I could quite honestly say, "I haven't plans to do any of those things."

"Good. Now what did I come to the kitchen for? I know. To call Imogene Langley about the cake. She's going to make it, did I tell you? For Gloria's wedding?"

"How come?"

"Imogene is famous for her cakes. For the Williams girl — Tanya — she made one with a fountain. I didn't see it myself, but they say it was just beautiful."

I decided to change the subject. "Is Sylvia bringing Missy?"

"Missy? Why, of course. Why wouldn't she? Missy's not going to camp this summer." Mom got up and went to the phone. "Aren't you glad? Won't it be nice to see your little cousin again?"

"Missy's not my cousin. She's my niece."

"Isn't that what I just said?" Mom started dialing. She was getting as bad as Gloria, it seemed, but at least Mom had a good excuse for being absent-minded. "That you, Imogene? Alice."

It was kind of weird, having a niece just about a year younger than me. That's what comes, though, from having a real old sister. Missy got a charge out of calling me "Uncle" sometimes. I thought it was pretty funny myself.

Mom started talking about the cake, so I got up and left.

As I was getting ready for bed I thought of Missy and her great ideas. She had a really good imagination, or maybe it was just that she read a lot.

One time we put up a tent right in the screened-in porch and had a kerosene lamp and sleeping bags, and told spook stories. That Missy could talk blood and thunder with the best of them.

One time, too, we pretended the whole area was flooded. We sat on the roof, as though waiting to be rescued. Missy was carrying on, wringing her hands and saying we'd probably never live to see another dawn, when someone slowed down in their car and then took off. The next thing we knew, the fire department was there to rescue us with ladders, like you would a cat up a tree. My parents weren't too thrilled about that. Later, though, when Sylvia drove down to get Missy, we heard them tell her about our escapade and they were laughing.

This time, though, Sylvia would be around to blow the whistle. She didn't find things funny the way my parents did. I guess being divorced had taken some of the good nature out of her. She didn't kid around a whole lot. *Kid.* There was that word again.

If Missy were here and I'd said the word *kid* out loud, she'd have cranked her elbow against mine and said, "Honk honk." Missy loves a play on words, and she always does the *honk honk* thing when she hears one. I've learned to do it, too.

I'd have too much on my mind, though, to fool around with kid stuff (ignore the *kid*, I told myself) when Missy and Sylvia arrived on Sunday. First, I'd have to keep Rudy contented so he wouldn't make a big fuss and raise trouble. What had Oliver said? Goats are friendly and need companionship. "Prince, you're going to be on duty," I said.

Hearing his name, the dog came sniffing around. I scratched him under the muzzle. "I know how you like being in my room and all, Prince, but for a while you may have to sleep out in the clubhouse with Rudy."

Prince gave a little moan.

"Hey, you won't mind, will you?" I pulled out the third drawer down in my desk and found a stale Milky Way bar, one of the little ones, from last Halloween. Before I even had a chance to unwrap it, Prince scarfed it down, paper and all. "You like that, huh? Well, let me tell you, Prince. There are more where that one came from."

Prince slobbered all over my wrist, trying to get me to hand over more treats. He gave a few eager yipes.

"Knock it off," I said, "or I'll put you outside right now."

As though he understood me, old dumb Prince flattened himself against the door and made little moaning sounds while rolling his eyes. I had my doubts about his being a good buddy to the goat. The least little thing turned Prince into practically a mental case.

"Honey, you didn't have to get up so early, just because I'm leaving," Mom said to me the next morning. "There's no need to worry. I'll be home in a few days."

"I'm not worried about *that*."

She gave my chin a little squeeze. "And your aunt Harriet will be fine." She frowned. "I hope."

I felt like a real creep. It wasn't either of those things that made me twitchy.

"What are your plans for today?" Dad asked, coming out to the kitchen.

"Well . . . Woody's coming over." Mom and Dad both thought Woody was a fine young man. They always said he was so polite and grown-up.

"That's nice," Mom said now. "Woody's so polite and grown-up."

After they left, I made myself breakfast. I had just finished off the second open-faced peanut butter and marshmallow creme sandwich when Woody came to the back door. I yelled for him to come in.

"Come, come, my good man, no dawdling," he said, tapping a rolled paper against my shoulder.

"What's that?"

"Plans for building the feeder. I copied them out of a book at the library. Animal husbandry is a fascinating subject." And then, even though I didn't ask, he explained that animal husbandry was the study of animal raising.

We went over to Frank's. He was waiting for us out by the shed.

"Let's see those plans," Frank said. He made a big deal about looking them over. "We'll need some one-by-twos," he said after a bit. "And some two-by-fours." He pulled out several long pieces of wood. "And we'll need a saw, nails, and a hammer. All right, grab this stuff, you guys, and let's get moving."

We went down the incline in back of Frank's place

and then walked along the creek to the clubhouse.

"I gather your folks don't know about the goat yet, Frank," Woody said.

"You gather right."

"I plan it as a surprise for my own parents," Woody said amiably. "They're often after me to do something physical, like taking hikes. I'll probably hike down this way a lot, once Rudy gets here."

"Did you tell your folks?" Frank asked me.

"Not yet. It wasn't a good time." I stopped to get a better grip on the lumber without getting splinters in my fingers.

"Come on," Woody said, watching me shift the lumber. "We'll never be finished if we don't snap things up a little."

I heaved the wood under my arm and trotted along after Frank, who was loaded down with tools. Woody, bringing up the rear, was carrying . . . what was he carrying? Just a box of nails. Boy, was that typical!

CHAPTER 4

Money Troubles Ahead

I HAVE TO SAY Frank knew his onions when it came to building things. He measured everything and marked it and put Woody and me to work sawing. It wasn't too long before we had a shelf with slats nailed around it, ready to attach to the wall. It looked quite a bit like the feeder in the sketch Woody had brought along.

"Which wall should we nail it on?" I asked Frank.

"That one." He pointed it out. "Just under the window's a good place for it."

The window was the old kind that swings up and fastens to the wall with a little hook. We had it raised now, to give more ventilation.

"How high should we put the feeder?" Woody asked.

Frank scratched his head. "I can't picture how tall

Rudy is. We don't want the shelf too high for him. But if it's too low, he might rake the food around with his hoof."

"Hold it against the wall, you guys," Woody said. "So we can estimate."

We did.

"Higher. No, that's too high. Hmmm, now that's too low, I think." Woody stepped back as far as he could. "Frank, can you hold up the shelf again? Good. Now, Doug, pretend you're the goat."

"What? Come on!"

"Seriously. Get down on all fours."

I looked at each of them, but neither one seemed about to laugh. "Oh, all right. But make it quick." I got down. I felt like a fool.

"Now raise your head and see if you can reach over the slat and get at the food."

I tried, but my neck wouldn't stretch that far. "It needs to be lower."

"For you, maybe," Frank said. "I'm not so sure about Rudy. Lift up a little, Doug, on your hind legs."

That did it. I got up. "I'm not really into playing goat," I said.

Woody patted my shoulder. "You did just fine, Doug. Okay, let's put the shelf about there, where you have it now, Frank."

After we'd finished, we stood around congratulating ourselves on the neat job we'd done. The shelf was plenty big enough for feed and for the salt block. The water would be in a bucket on the floor.

"The next thing we need is bedding," Woody said.

"Bedding?" Frank looked about to laugh.

"I'm not talking designer sheets or quilts," Woody told us. "Just something to keep Rudy off this . . . uh . . . ground." The clubhouse had no floor, but the dirt had been pounded down solidly through the years.

I told them we had some old pieces of indoor-outdoor carpeting, so we went up to my house.

My sister Gloria was sitting at the kitchen table sipping her Cran-Apple juice and leafing through a bride's magazine.

"Oh, hi, sweetie," she said, giving me her vacant smile. "I wondered where you were. Oh, and hello, sweetie," she said to Woody. Woody beamed.

"This is Frank," I said, nodding toward him. "The one who moved into the Werth house."

"Oh, well, welcome to the neighborhood!" She half rose, and I thought for an awful moment she was going to give Frank a kiss on the cheek. Instead, though, she got all the way up and poured herself some more juice. "Anyone want some?" she asked, holding up the container. "It's real good."

"We just came in to get something," I said. "Come on, guys, the stuff is down in the basement."

Only Frank followed me. When we staggered back upstairs, carrying the scraps of carpet, Woody was seated at the table with Gloria, their heads bent over a picture in the magazine. Gloria looked up. "Woody agrees that this kind of bouquet is just right for the gown I'll be wearing at my wedding," she said.

"It's simple, yet it makes a statement," Woody said.

"Yeah, I could make a statement, too," I said, glaring

at him. "How about giving us a hand here?"

"At your service." Woody stood and made a little bow for Gloria's benefit.

"Oh, you are the cutest thing," she said, dimpling. "I could just hug you to pieces!"

Woody shyly lowered his head. His ears had turned a bright red.

I heard Frank making gurgling sounds. "C'mon, let's get going," I said.

We took the carpet down to the shed. After trying to fit pieces together for quite a while, we finally got the ground covered. Although we knew we might have to change rugs later if these got too messed up, we decided to take all the extras back to the basement for the time being.

Gloria was gone. Her friend Tricia had probably picked her up. I couldn't keep track of Gloria's hours at the beauty shop. Some days she worked until seven or eight at night.

I poured out some milk for the guys and passed around a box of cookies.

Prince shambled into the kitchen. "Hello, mutt," I said. "I knew you'd come around for your share." To the guys I said, "He'll eat anything. He's worse than a goat."

Woody gave a little gasp. "Oh no! Oh no, I'd forgotten!"

"About Prince's appetite?" Why should that upset Woody?

"No, no! About Rudy . . . the food for Rudy! Remember what Oliver said? Not that he'd provide food, but that he'd sell it to us. Cheap. I wonder what he calls *cheap*."

Frank looked worried. "To that guy it could mean a hundred dollars. Hey — maybe we'd better back out of this while we have the chance!"

I was torn two ways. I could see myself in deep financial trouble — as well as other kinds — and yet I really didn't want to give up on the idea of having Rudy for two whole weeks. "Maybe we could call Oliver and ask how much?"

"Excellent idea." To my relief Woody went to the phone himself to make the call. When he got Oliver on the line, he said, "You'll be glad to hear, Oliver, that the guys and I have Rudy's quarters all ready. Feed bin and everything. Speaking of feed — I mean, fodder — you're going to bring it?"

There was a pause while Woody listened. His ears reddened. "You must be kidding," he finally gasped. "I thought we were friends. Surely you don't —" There was a long pause while he listened some more. Finally he said, "No, no, I understand. Of course. I'll explain it to the club members. See you then. With the goat."

When he hung up he was perspiring. "I couldn't get him to come down," he said. "You heard how I tried."

"How much, how much?" Frank demanded.

"Eleven fifty. No more, no less."

"I don't even have the fifty," Frank said.

"Hey, come on," I yelled. "Now's a fine time to tell us!"

"No one asked me before!" Frank looked mad. "So make something of it!"

"Don't you guys start in now," Woody said, slumping into a kitchen chair. "We've got enough problems without that." He drummed his fingers on the table. "Eleven fifty. Plus the three fifty." He brightened. "Of course, we won't pay the three fifty per week until afterward, when they come to take Rudy back. So eleven fifty is all we'll need on Saturday. I believe I can bankroll it for the time being. Until the money starts flowing in."

"Flowing in from where?" I wanted to know.

Woody had regained his good spirits. "I have ideas. Ideas of how we can make this venture with Rudy pay off."

"Tell us," I said.

Woody stood up, all confidence now. "I've got to work out the details in my mind," he said. "In the meantime, we'll have to find a tarp. A tarpaulin, you know. To cover the feed . . . fodder. Oliver wishes we had a separate building to store the fodder in, but he's being reasonable about it. Oh, and he said to have the stake ready."

Frank gasped. "Steak? Rudy eats steak?"

"Stake, stupid. S-t-a-k-e. A thing you pound into the ground to tether the goat. If Rudy ran off, we'd be in a bunch of trouble."

With those words, my heart sank once again. Before, I had pictured Rudy lolling around at the clubhouse, waiting for us to come and play with him and being a load of fun and all. But now the scene changed. I could see Rudy running off — straight to some neighbor's garden.

"Yeah, well, you guys can worry about that," Frank said, strolling to the door. "I've got to go home and practice the tuba."

"And I should get home and do some heavy thinking," Woody said. "I'll put a tape of mood music or nature sounds into my Walkman. I always get good ideas when I'm plugged into it."

Frank just gave him a look and left.

Prince and I walked with Woody down to the clubhouse. He went on home, and I stepped inside the shed for another look around. I felt little tingles of excitement at the idea of having a real live goat there. "See, Prince?" I said as he came frisking inside. "Here's where you're going to be spending quite a bit of time. Sit."

Prince gave a few happy yelps and jiggled around.

"I said *sit*!"

Finally I pushed him down on his hind legs. Prince flopped all the way, then half turned and rolled his eyes.

"I don't think I've ever seen a dumber dog," I told him. I backed up a bit. "Now *stay*."

Prince rolled all the way over.

"Stay." I backed up more, all the way out of the door. "Stay. Good dog." I fastened the new padlock Woody had brought. I'd leave Prince inside for about an hour, just to get him used to the idea. Apparently, he didn't mind. After one or two yipes he was quiet.

Going back up the incline and through the yard, I felt that earlier uneasiness come over me again. There were going to be more problems to this goat business than I had thought. The main one was what to tell my parents. If this thing got out of control, it wasn't going to help one bit that there were three guys involved. There were also three sets of parents. Potentially angry parents.

But still, there was no real cause for worry. Was there? Wouldn't Mom and Dad be pleased to have me busy with something and not underfoot, what with Gloria's wedding about to come off? If they looked at it from that angle, they'd have to admit their son had shown a lot of initiative.

I reached the door to the screened-in porch, but didn't go in. Something was wrong. It was just too quiet. Prince should have been howling up a storm by this time. He raised a ruckus every time we locked him in the house when we were going somewhere. Down there, he'd be even worse.

I turned back and headed for the clubhouse. I got to the edge of the incline and looked down just in time to see Prince come leaping through the window. Wow. How could he jump so high? And then I knew. He'd managed to get up to the feed bin and from there had made the leap through the window.

In some ways Prince wasn't so dumb at all.

CHAPTER 5

Love at First Sniff

GLORIA WAS WORKING late that night and then going out, so Dad and I ate alone. All we had to do was heat up some leftovers.

"What have you been doing all day?" Dad asked as he spooned the food into a dish.

"Fixing up the clubhouse. With Frank and Woody."

"It's amazing," he said, "how that old shack has stood up all these years. Did I ever tell you how we — the fathers — came to build it?"

As a matter of fact, he had. Hundreds of times. But I let him tell it again. Sylvia, he said, was a kid at the time, and there were about eight or ten others, right in the neighborhood. Dad went on to name the kids, mostly, I think, just to see if he could still remember.

After he got through, I said, "Larry Williams . . . wasn't he the one who was crazy about Sylvia?"

"That's right. And it was mutual. We always thought

the two of them would get married someday, settle down here." Dad got up to get the coffeepot. Pouring, he continued, "But Sylvia insisted on going away to college, where she could major in art. Well, she never came back. Young Williams stayed around, though. That is, after he finished law school."

Dad set down his cup. "It's strange," he said. "At the last Elks meeting, Larry asked me about Sylvia. I have the feeling he never got over her. He was married, had a couple of kids, but got divorced a year or so ago." He paused. "And Sylvia's divorced, too."

It was almost as though Dad was thinking they might get together again. I felt a little uncomfortable, as if I were seeing into his mind and he didn't notice. "Is she coming here for sure Sunday?" I asked. "And Missy?"

Just then the phone rang. It was like a psychic experience, because Sylvia was on the other end. "Wow," I said. "We were just talking about you, Dad and I."

"Oh? Good or bad?" She gave a little laugh and said, "I just wanted to double-check if Mother got off, and if you're still expecting us."

"Well, sure. What time will you get here Sunday?"

"Around noon, I should think. We're driving. Here's Missy to say hello. Now, Doug, keep it brief. My phone bill's sky-high as it is."

Missy came on. "Hi, Uncle Doug!"

"Hi, niece! Hey, are we going to have fun!" I glanced around. Dad had left the room. With lowered voice I said, "There's going to be something new going on at the clubhouse."

"What?"

"Can't tell. It'll knock your socks off, though."

"I can't wait! Maybe I'll coax so we can come tomorrow."

"No, don't do that. It won't be ready. We have to do things first."

"Oh, please, give me a hint." There was a voice in the background — Sylvia's. Missy said, "I have to hang up now. Oh, I can't wait. 'Bye!"

My big sister would probably ask Missy what we were talking about, but I knew I could count on the kid to be cool about it. Missy was the only person on earth who could handle Sylvia.

There are several advantages to having a father who works for the local newspaper. He knows the ins and outs of everything going on in town, even if he doesn't write about it. I've heard some pretty good scandals in my day. Another thing is, he works odd hours. Like today, he wasn't hanging around the house like a lot of fathers do on Saturday. He was gone, and Gloria was still asleep when Woody called.

"All set for G-Day?" he asked.

"I guess." I got a feeling in the pit of my stomach. "Woody, are you sure we should go through with this?"

"Why, Doug, you surprise me. Surely you're not having second thoughts?"

Actually it was about umpteenth thoughts. "I can't help thinking of all the things that could go wrong."

"Doug, I'm not going to ask you what those things

are, because I don't want to encourage negative thoughts. Look, the shed is ready, we're ready. Frank's bringing over an iron stake. Oliver — and I checked this out — will deliver Rudy at eleven or so. And the feed.

"Now, Doug, don't let the money thing dampen your spirits. As I said before, I can bankroll it for the time being. I just cleaned up on my birthday."

"Okay." I had some money, too, but probably not enough. "Hurry on over, will you? I'm pretty nervous here, alone and all. And bring Frank. He's in on this too."

I called Prince and we went down to the clubhouse. At first he whined and got stiff-legged when I tried to shove him inside, but he calmed down when I went in and sat on the carpet. "You might as well get used to it, buddy," I said. "You're going to spend a lot of time in here." I checked the window. It was closed all right, and hooked.

I knew the guys were close by when Prince began barking. He was a really good watchdog. I had to tell him to shut up a few times, though, when the guys came inside. He just didn't know when to stop.

"I've got the stake," Frank said. "And a mallet to pound it in with. I'd better do that now." He left, and Prince, now palsy, frisked along with Frank.

We got a bucket up at the house and filled it with water and brought it down. "Rudy could probably drink from the creek," Woody said, "but we wouldn't want him to get his feet wet. And get pneumonia. And die on us."

Something else to worry about.

We went up to the house and hung around out front. After quite a while we saw a truck slow down, stop, then turn into our driveway. My heart began beating like anything.

Oliver was leaning his head over the side of the truck bed. Country-western music blared away. It sounded even louder once the engine was turned off.

"Would you turn that durn thing off!" Oliver's dad yelled as he got out of the truck.

Sudden silence. Oliver shimmied over the side of the truck. "Rudy likes country tunes, Pa," he said.

"Yeah, well I'm not interested in what that goat likes." He eyed us. "You the boys going to look after the animal?"

"We certainly are," Woody said. The red was creeping up in his ears. "This is an exciting moment for us, sir." We all walked to the back of the truck.

Oliver's father looked a bit perplexed. "Is something going on?"

"They're excited about the goat, Pa," Oliver said. "They've never had a goat before."

"That so?" The man looked as though this was some kind of unusual thing. "Well, nothing to it. Just feed him and keep his place clean and leave him to romp around. He lowered the back end of the truck and took hold of a chain. "Come on, goat," he said. "Get moving."

Rudy lifted his head and sniffed this way and that, as though checking out the atmosphere.

"I said *git*!" Oliver's dad gave the chain a snap. There

was a terrible moment when I wondered what he'd do if . . . but then Rudy very deliberately leaped to the ground. *Maa . . . aa . . . aa!*

"Here, take this," the man said, handing me the chain, "while we get out the fodder. Come on, Oliver, look smart."

As I stood there holding the chain, Rudy looked me over.

I'm not going to be like Oliver, I wanted to say, *putting on a big show, but probably not caring all that much about you. I'll look after you really well and see that you're happy while you're here.*

Rudy appeared to pick up my thoughts. He blinked his eyes at me and made a funny little sideways motion with his jaw. He almost seemed to be saying, *Forget those clowns over there. You and I are special. We're going to have a secret understanding.*

"You sure are special," I murmured, leaning down to him. Rudy nuzzled my cheek.

Meanwhile, Oliver and his dad had tossed out four bales of fodder and a huge sack that had *Peanut Shells* printed on it. "This," Oliver said, "is to spread on the floor, to catch the manure. Then you can scoop it all out together. Makes great fertilizer, right, Pa?"

"If you can keep any kind of garden with a dang goat on the premises," the father said. "Here's what's left of the salt block. I'll throw that in free of charge. Speaking of *charge* . . ." He got out a scrap of paper. "Feed comes to eleven fifty."

"Here you are," Woody said, handing over the money.

Oliver's dad got a sly look, as though he had put something over on us. He counted the money and shoved it in his pocket. "That goat shouldn't give you any trouble. What you've got to do is show him who's boss. C'mon, Oliver." He got into the truck.

"Pa," Oliver yelled, "don't you want me to make sure they fixed up that shed the way I told them to?"

"We've got no time for that," his father said. "Now get in this truck, boy, or forget about taking the trip."

"Okay, just let me get my radio." Oliver reached into the back of the truck and pulled out a small portable. "You guys make sure you take good care of Rudy," he said, climbing into the front seat. Over the sound of the starting engine he yelled, "And don't let him get lonesome or you'll be sorry!"

His father backed out and they took off down the street.

It had happened so suddenly. The truck had arrived, it was unloaded, and then it was gone. Only now Rudy was standing here.

"Wow! We've got him!" Woody exclaimed. "We've really got Rudy!"

"Yeah." I could hardly believe it. We were all pretty excited; Rudy was the only one who seemed calm.

"Hi, fella," I said, scratching him under the chin. "Are you all set for a nice little visit?" He brushed against me as if to say, *I'm ready if you are.*

"Look at Prince," Frank said. "He doesn't know what to make of all this."

Prince was crawling forward, eyes widened, deep growling sounds coming from his throat. Rudy flicked his head, and Prince, with a yipe, spun around and took off. Then he began crawling forward again.

"You nerd," I said. "Not you, Rudy. Prince."

"Let's get going," Frank said. "I'll take Rudy on down to the clubhouse and you guys can bring the fodder." He took the chain and said, "Come on, Rudy." But the goat stood stiff-legged and refused to move.

"I said come on!" Frank said, giving the chain a snap.

"Don't do that!" I went to Rudy and leaned down to put my face next to his. "Don't be afraid, boy," I told him. "We really will be good to you. We'll even bring you leftovers."

Rudy gave a little *maa . . . aa* sound, brushed against me, and as I began walking he trotted along beside me.

"Incredible," Woody murmured as we made our way down the incline. "That goat has taken a shine to you, Doug."

"Maybe he has the same smell as Oliver," Frank said. "Or else maybe Doug smells like another goat."

"Hey!" I'd have decked Frank for that, only I didn't want to upset Rudy. "Just watch your mouth, Frank."

"Now, fellas," Woody said. "We're all excited, but let's remember we're gentlemen." We were now near the shed. "Let's fasten Rudy to the stake and then we'll bring down the supplies."

We kept the tether short so that, in case Rudy got upset or jumpy, he couldn't go far. He seemed at ease, though, gazing around, checking out the location.

Prince was the hyper one. He kept circling around, giving sharp barks, but keeping well away from Rudy.

"I hate to insult your dog," Frank said to me, "but he's some kind of nut."

Secretly I agreed, but I said, "Prince is just worked up."

We decided to take turns, one guy staying with Prince and Rudy while the other two brought down the supplies. We put some fodder into the feeder inside and stacked the rest on the other side of the shed, beyond the reach of Rudy's chain. Then we covered it with the tarp and weighted down the edges with rocks.

Through all of this, Rudy watched with an interested gaze. He sure was friendly. He not only let us scratch him under the chin and pet him, but as soon as we stopped, he'd nuzzle us to do it some more.

After a while Rudy started nibbling on weeds and grass, as far as his chain would reach. He certainly had a good appetite.

"As I was sitting in my room, yesterday, earphones in place, a great idea flowed into my mind," Woody said. "About goats. You know, they're like living lawn-mowers."

"I don't get it," Frank said. "So goats eat grass. Big deal."

Woody smiled at Frank the way his professor father probably smiled at dense students. "Think, Frank. Goats eat grass. They love it. People cut grass. They hate it. So, if we put the two together, what do we have?"

Frank looked confused.

"I see you understand," Woody said. "We rent Rudy

out to eat — and thereby cut — people's grass. And by doing so we make big money."

"That's right!" Frank said.

Rent out Rudy? There was something about that idea that bothered me, but I didn't know what.

Judging from the smiles of the others, though, there didn't seem to be a problem. I guess I was just a little hyper myself, from so much going on with my family — Aunt Harriet's operation, and Mom being gone, and Gloria getting married, and Missy and Sylvia coming to stay. And now, having a goat practically in my backyard and none of my family knowing about it.

But everything would work out fine. All I had to do was keep cool up at the house and act as though nothing unusual was going on.

And in the meantime, I'd be spending hours down here with this really great goat who was smart as a whip. Hadn't he picked up right away on the idea that I was his friend? That I'd protect him?

He sure had. So there was really no problem at all.

At least none that I wanted to think of just now.

CHAPTER 6

A Surprise for Missy

ON SUNDAY MORNING I felt like the dickens. It had been a bad night. Prince, not one bit thrilled about being shut up in the shed with Rudy, had nearly howled his head off.

Each time he began a new series of sounds I sat up and listened. Dad seemed not to hear, though. It was lucky that his room, and also Gloria's, were in the front of the house. Also those rooms, which got blasted by the afternoon sun, had window fans that kicked up quite a bit of noise.

Eventually, though, if the howls kept on long enough, Dad and Gloria would be sure to hear them. I had to do something. I got up, pulled jeans on over my pajamas, grabbed a flashlight, and went down to the shed.

Prince jumped all over me when I entered it, but Rudy just raised his head as though to say, *Don't blame me*.

"Hey, fella," I told him, "you're okay. I'll just take Mr. Noisy-Britches here and let you get some sleep." Rudy lowered his head and gave the tiniest of goat sighs.

Once inside my room, Prince calmed down and got some shut-eye, but at about 6:00 A.M. Rudy started *maa-aa*ing. I hoped this was just because he was in a strange place and not his usual wake-up time.

I'm not great for early rising, especially in the summer. This morning, though, I went down to keep Rudy company. He shut up as soon as I walked into the shed. Because it was smelly in there, I took him outside and kept him company until breakfasttime.

When we were sitting at the table Gloria said, "Doug, honey, you look terrible. Is something wrong? Do you miss Mom that much?"

"I miss her, but I didn't stay awake crying last night, if that's what you mean."

Dad lowered the editorial section of the Chicago Sunday paper. He always checked out what he called his competition, even though his paper was just a suburban weekly. "It seemed to me I heard howling last night," he said. "Is there a new dog in the neighborhood?"

I hesitated a moment and then said, "It was Prince. I left him out last night and he didn't like it."

"Oh. It seems to me he should be outside. That's

where a watchdog belongs." Dad went back to the paper.

Prince, the coward of the canines, would never make it as a watchdog, I thought, but I didn't say it. Instead I asked Gloria what time Missy and Sylvia were due to arrive.

"Sometime after lunch. Sylvia said not to bother cooking up a storm, they'd stop somewhere along the way."

"What about dinner tonight?" Dad said over the top of the newspaper.

"Oh." Gloria thought hard. "I could make hamburger delight."

"There's no need to tie yourself up with cooking," Dad said. "We can eat out."

"You're sure? All right," Gloria said. "I have so much on my mind as it is."

As soon as I could, I excused myself, saying the guys were going to meet down at the clubhouse.

Both Woody and Frank were there. Rudy was happily munching away on weeds. "Hey, Rudy," I said. "Come see your pal from last night." That goat acted like he understood. He came to me and playfully butted against my side. I scratched him under the chin. Then I told the guys what had gone on last night.

"Prince will get used to keeping Rudy company," Woody said. "Look at him now."

Oh, sure. Now that there was no need for it, Prince was giving Rudy these looks of true love and companionship. He'd do his famous belly crawl and then pounce up with a happy bark, as though to say, *Don't you think I'm cute?* Rudy would stop chewing and look at Prince, I swear, with a smile on his face. Goats have a natural smiley look, though.

"Have you sprung the news on your family yet?" Frank asked me. "About the goat?"

"No way. If Mom was here, maybe I would. I can talk her into most things, and then she talks Dad into them. With her gone, though, I can't take the chance."

"At my house it's just the opposite," Frank said. "Mom rules the roost. What about you, Woody?"

"I can pretty well handle either one of my parents. I didn't tell them about Rudy, though, because of you two gentlemen. Parents do talk to each other, you know."

"Yeah," I agreed. "Let's all of us keep it quiet for a while. Until Rudy gets settled and calmed down and all. I don't want to give my dad any cause for complaint."

"That sounds logical," Woody said. "First let's get Rudy trained to a routine that will make him a golden example of the goat species." He pulled a pair of rubber gloves from his hip pocket and put them on. "I came prepared to take the first turn in cleaning out the floor of the shed. We're all in this together."

Woody picked up a shovel that was leaning against the shack and stepped inside. He stepped out fast, looking as though he might toss his cookies. He took a deep breath, though, and picked up a garbage bag. "Hold this, someone, while I scoop it out," he said.

Frank jumped up and held the bag. Woody shoveled

46

peanut shells and pitched them into the bag.

"There's a twister stuck to the bag," Woody said when he was finished. "Just twist it up and leave the bag behind the clubhouse, Frank."

Woody stripped off his gloves, the way doctors do after surgery on TV, and turned to me. "Doug, when the bags get full, be sure to put them in front of your house for the garbage collector."

"If there's a bunch of them by next Thursday, I'm not going to put them all out. It would look suspicious."

"Divide them, why don't you, among your neighbors." That Woody. He always had an answer for everything.

We took Rudy for a little walk along the creek and messed around for a while, and then we all had to leave for lunch. Rudy, fastened to the stake, looked contented and pleased. Prince lay down near him.

"You two," I said before I left. "I don't want to hear a peep out of you. Or rather, a bark or a bleat." They gazed at me, all innocence.

Lunch was grilled cheese sandwiches, slightly burnt. I'd be glad to have Sylvia around for one reason. She was a good cook.

It was about two when they drove up. Sylvia had her dark hair in one big fat braid down her back and some kind of beaded band around her head. It made me think of Pocahontas. She hugged and kissed all of us.

Missy was wearing her old camp T-shirt and jeans. Her dark hair was longer than ever, almost to her waist. We gave each other the old hand clasp and how-deedo. Dad and Gloria kissed her, though, and Dad called her "little sweetheart."

Dad and I carried the luggage upstairs. Sylvia was going to share Gloria's room. Missy got Sylvia's old room, at the back of the house, next to mine.

Everyone sat around yakking for a while. I knew Missy was waiting, the same as I was, for the right time to split. The time came when they started talking about the wedding. Then Missy said, "I've got a surprise for you, Doug. It's in my room. Let me go up first, and then you come and stand in the hall outside my door. Okay?"

"Okay." I was dying to tell her about Rudy, but I thought, *Let her do the little surprise first. It'll knock her socks off when she hears about mine.*

In a few minutes I went up and tapped on her door. Silence. Then a *maa-aa-aa* sound! I almost flipped out. How could she have done it? How could she have sneaked Rudy into the house and upstairs without any of us hearing? I didn't think she'd even been out of the room!

The sound came again. "*Maa-aa-aa.*" I rattled the doorknob. "Missy?"

"Okay. Come in."

I did. She was standing there alone, a smile on her face. No sign of Rudy.

"What . . . ?" I looked around.

Missy had a little round object in her hand. She turned it over. A *maa-aa-aa* sound came out of it. I laughed in relief. "Where did you get that? I haven't seen one of those things in a long time."

"In a novelty shop. Doesn't it sound like a real cow, though?"

Cow. Oh. "Let's hear it again."

She turned it over. Yes, it did make a *moo-oo-oo*, not a *maa-aa-aa*.

"I brought it for you. As a surprise. It isn't much, but it's the thought that counts, as they say."

"Right. Keep it in your purse. Maybe we can fool the guys or something. Listen, I've got a surprise for you, too. It's a biggie." I told her about Rudy.

Missy's eyes widened with delight. "A real goat! Oh, come on, I've got to see it!"

We went through the backyard and down the incline. A tree growing near the clubhouse blocked it from view. When we reached the bottom, we saw the stake but not Rudy. His chain angled up from the stake. Following it with our eyes, we looked upward, and there was Rudy, still attached. He was stretched out on the clubhouse roof, staring at us with a look of amusement.

"My gosh!" I exclaimed. "How did he get up there?"

"How?" Missy said. "He jumped, of course. Goats are great jumpers. I did a report on a goat book one time. Come on down, baby," she said to Rudy. "Come and get acquainted."

Rudy just looked at her.

"I'll get something to coax him down," I said. I ran to the house and grabbed some carrots from the refrigerator. When I got back, Rudy was standing there by Missy, enjoying the joke, it seemed.

"Goats like to tease," Missy said. "Oh, Prince, are

you jealous?" That dumb dog was brushing against her and making whimpering sounds. Missy stooped down to pet Prince and tell him how wonderful he was. Prince rolled his eyes in that sappy way of his and flopped down on his stomach.

I held out the carrots toward Rudy. He came over, sniffed them, and started chomping. Every once in a while, though, he'd pause to nuzzle my arm. It gave me a really great feeling. It was as though Rudy was telling me that we were more than just boy and goat. We were friends. We did have a special understanding.

"Oh, poor Rudy," Missy said. "Just feel the weight of this chain." She held a section out to me. "Would you like something as heavy as this dragging on your neck, Doug? Would you?"

"No," I admitted. "But I'm not in the habit of jumping up on roofs, either." I looked at the goat. "Not that it stopped Rudy."

"I wish I'd brought my jump rope, to use instead," Missy said. "But anyway, it wouldn't be long enough. Shall I ask Grandpa if there's any . . . ? Oh, I guess I'd better not."

"That's right. Don't even *think* goat around the family. Not yet."

"You're right." Missy looked thoughtful. "We'll have to be very careful what we say for a day or two."

"Why a day or two?"

"Because after that they'll all be having such spazz attacks about the wedding, they won't pay any attention to us or what we're doing. It's always that way with my mom. I can get by with almost anything when she's racing to finish up one of her fashion lines. As long as I keep busy and out of the way, she leaves me alone. It'll be the same now. You'll see."

Missy was probably right. I felt a little easier. If we kept our lips zipped for a couple of days, we'd get by. As for Rudy's jumping . . . the only way to stop him would be to shorten the chain. Somehow I just couldn't do that, though. He had to have a little freedom when he was down here all alone. If jumping up on a roof was Rudy's idea of a good time, well, let him jump.

CHAPTER 7

It's Just a Joke,
Honk-Honk

SYLVIA MAY BE my big sister, but I don't think that gives her the right to be so critical. We were getting ready to go out for dinner when she said to me, "Doug, have you taken a bath since Mother left?"

"Why?"

"I hate to say this, Doug, but you *smell*. Or maybe it's your clothes. Have you changed them the last couple of days?"

"I don't know. I was going to get cleaned up anyway." I left. She really had a nerve, making personal comments like that. When I took off my jeans, though, I checked out around the cuffs. They did seem to smell a little of goat, but trust supernose Sylvia to make a federal case of it.

The restaurant we went to specialized in steak. My

sister and dad both ordered filets, but Missy and I insisted on hamburgers. "Please make mine rare," Missy told the waitress.

While we were eating salad and waiting for the main course, Sylvia and Dad got onto the subject I was really getting sick of hearing about. Gloria's wedding. Even though it was going to be a simple ceremony, in our garden, there were about a trillion things Sylvia thought should be done. She was still gabbing on about them when the waitress brought the big trayful of dinners. She handed out the steaks and then put down Missy's and my hamburgers.

Missy gave me a quick jab of her elbow — we were sitting side by side in the booth — took off the top half of bun, and then suddenly there was the *moo* sound! Missy looked up in pretend shock at the waitress. "I didn't want it *that* rare!" she exclaimed.

Sylvia, who had stopped midsentence at the sound of the cow, said, "All right, Missy. Not so very funny. Apologize!"

Missy smiled at the waitress. "It was just a joke," she said. "I'm sorry." She held up the *moo* box as an explanation.

When the waitress left, Sylvia said to Missy, "Is that why you ordered your hamburger rare? Just for that stupid joke?"

"I guess."

"Well, guess what. You're going to eat it. Whether you like it or not."

I have to give Missy credit. She ate that hamburger.

True, she smothered it in mustard, catsup, pickle, and tomato, even onion, but she did eat it. Missy's okay.

Later that night, she and I slipped away to see Rudy. When he saw me he made little sounds and leaped over and nuzzled me. "Hi, pal," I said, putting him into the shed. "Are you going to be a good goat and keep quiet tonight?"

It didn't seem like it. As soon as we left, Rudy started bleating.

There was no point in putting Prince in with Rudy. It would just double the noise. "I have a weird feeling I may have to go down and sleep in the clubhouse tonight," I told Missy.

"Then so will I."

"No. Your mom won't check on me, but she may on you, tonight. She'd have a fit if you turned up missing."

"It would be nice if you could let Rudy know you're not far away, and there's nothing to worry about."

"Yeah. Well, I don't know goat talk."

"I've got an idea, Doug. Of what to do if Rudy bleats. Just pretend it's the moo box. Every time Rudy goes *maa-aaa*, make the cow box go *moo-ooo*."

"Good idea."

For a while the TV drowned out all other sound, but when we went up to bed, I heard a bleat coming from the direction of the clubhouse. I turned over the cow box. *Moo-oo*! It was good my room and Missy's were the only ones facing the backyard.

After an hour or so passed and Rudy was still giving a bleat now and then, followed by my *moo* sounds, Sylvia rapped on my door and came in. "Doug, I know you're young, but are you *that* young? To play with a baby toy all night long? Would you please put it away? Honestly!"

I didn't say what I wanted to say. After she left, though, I switched into a high-pitched voice and mocked her: "I know you're young, but are you *that* young?" She really got my goat. *Got my goat.* It was funny how often goats and kids came into conversations. But back to Sylvia. She treated me as though I were a little kid instead of a kid brother. Making me change clothes. I would have anyway. *Clothes!* That gave me an idea. My jeans might smell of goat, but also, to a goat, they would smell of *me.* If I took my T-shirt and jeans down to Rudy, maybe he'd quiet down, thinking I was near.

I fished my clothes out of the hamper. Then, very quietly, I went downstairs, grabbed the flashlight, and walked down the slope to Rudy.

He was so glad to see me it was pathetic. I mean, it was as though his best friend had deserted him and then come back. And now that I was there, Prince came trotting after me, acting as though he'd been on the job all along.

I put my clothes into a little pile just inside the club-house and let Rudy sniff them. He moved them around with his hoof, like a chicken making a nest. When they were arranged to his satisfaction, he lowered himself onto them.

Then old Prince had to go over and sniff, too.

I backed away. The two were sitting there, with Rudy not budging one bit. Prince pawed at one pants leg, pulled it free, and then sat on it. They looked pretty funny. It made me feel proud, though, to realize they thought so much of me they'd lay claim to my old, dirty clothes. No matter what Sylvia thought, smells were good things to have at times.

When I got back upstairs I leaned on the windowsill and listened. There was a little bleat now and then but nothing to keep people awake. It looked as though I might get a good night's sleep myself.

I awakened to the smell of bacon frying. Mom would be calling me in a minute. And then I remembered. Mom was gone. Sylvia. Goat. *Goat!*

I leaped out of bed and listened. No sound from outside. Maybe Rudy had decided to sleep in. Maybe he'd gotten loose and run away!

It took me just a couple of minutes to toss on my clothes. I raced downstairs and toward the kitchen and . . . wow. They were all there — Sylvia, Missy, Gloria, my dad.

"Well, sleepyhead," Sylvia said. "I was about to go up and drag you out." She smiled. "Sit down. I've got your pancakes in the warming oven."

Trapped. I sat down and looked over at Missy, who was just draining the last of her milk. She blotted her lips daintily and, after a quick glance around, gave a slight nod of her head toward the backyard and then circled a finger in the air as an okay sign.

I was really relieved. I found out later that my niece had gotten up early and had gone out and sweet-talked Rudy and given him some fodder.

The phone rang. If it was Woody, I'd have to put him off.

It was Mom.

Dad talked to her awhile and then Sylvia. Then Missy got on the line. It still made me feel funny to hear Missy call my mother Grandma.

"What's going on?" I asked my father. "Is Aunt Harriet all right?"

"No, as a matter of fact, it sounds more serious than we thought. They need to operate, but your aunt is too weak to go through that right now."

"So is Mom coming home or what?"

"We told her to stay on," Sylvia told me. "There's no use in her coming home and then going right back. Besides, she feels needed. It's a comfort to all of them to have Mother there."

"Poor Mother," Gloria said with a sigh. "Poor Aunt Harriet." She wrinkled her pretty brow. "And poor me."

"Poor you?" Now Sylvia's brow was wrinkled. "Why poor you?"

Gloria delivered a sigh. "Because I don't know what I'll do about getting married without Mother to see to things."

Sylvia looked concerned. "Gloria, it's less than two weeks until the wedding. Have you made any decisions at all?"

"Oh, right," Gloria said. "On our honeymoon we're going to . . . oh, I'm not supposed to tell, am I?"

"I'm talking about the *ceremony*," Sylvia said. "Flowers, cake, punch, champagne. Have you and Mother done anything at all about them? Is there a list some-where?"

"Yes, I believe there is," Gloria said, getting up. "I'll just go and find it."

Sylvia passed her hand over her face, then rested her chin on her hand and looked at me. "What are your plans for today, Doug?"

Boy, I wasn't prepared for that one. "What do you mean — *plans?*"

"I can't see children just aimlessly wasting away their summers. They should be doing something construc-tive."

"I am," I said. And without really thinking about it, I added, "I'm learning about animal husbandry."

"You're what?"

"Learning about the care and feeding of . . . of . . ."

"I know the meaning of the term, Doug, but . . . oh, I see you found the list, Gloria," she said.

"Yes," Gloria sighed. "There's a lot to do." She sat down and handed the list to Sylvia. "But just don't blame Mother. She was doing the best she could. It's not her fault if . . ."

Sylvia didn't answer. We've all heard her in the past, though, giving advice to Mom about doing things right away instead of putting them off until later. Sylvia herself is superorganized. Personally, I like Mom the way she is, easygoing. At least she's pleasant to be around.

"I see your dress is crossed off the list," Sylvia said to Gloria. "You have it, then, I presume?"

"Not exactly." Gloria scooped up a bit of strawberry

jam from the edge of the jar and licked her finger. "Something was wrong. Oh, I remember. It didn't fit. They sent off for the right size, though."

"What about the bridesmaids?"

"Oh, Tricia and Alice are all set. They're really excited."

"I mean their dresses. Do you have them?"

"No, they have them."

"I see. And are they all right?"

"Sure. They picked them out themselves. Tricia's has a lot of ruffles and Alice's . . . let's see." Gloria thought hard. "Alice's is kind of scoop-necked. Yellow. And Tricia's is peach."

Sylvia looked at Gloria as though she couldn't believe all this. "Are you saying the girls picked out their own dresses, without any regard for the total effect?"

"Oh, they're nice dresses," Gloria said. "The peach was even on sale."

I remembered one time when Sylvia said, "It's amazing. The world's three biggest featherheads all born in the same town — and friends." She looked as though she was thinking the same thing again.

"I believe we'll schedule a little fashion session," Sylvia said with a sigh. "See how those dresses go together — if they do at all, which I doubt. And the bride's dress. I'd like to see at least the sample that you ordered from."

"Oh, fun!" Gloria said, looking thrilled. "And Missy's dress, too. We've got to get that."

"Missy's?"

"Sure. Don't you remember, I told you a long time

ago that I wanted Missy to be a junior bridesmaid."

"Yes, I remember that," Missy said. "And I told you, Gloria, that I'd just love to. Remember, Mother?"

I could see that my big sister didn't remember at all, but she wasn't about to admit it. "It's a bit late now. . . ."

"Oh, please!" Missy coaxed. "Gloria's my one and only aunt!"

"Then suppose you try calling her *Aunt* Gloria," Sylvia said.

"Yes'm." Missy looked up through her bangs, hardly able to keep from smiling. She'd won the junior bridesmaid round.

Gloria turned to me. "Oh, Dougie," she coaxed, taking my chin in her hand. "Won't you change your mind and be in the wedding, too? You'd look so adorable!"

I jerked away from her hand. "Nothing doing!" I could feel my face flame just knowing that the family had heard what she said. If the guys had been there, I'd have croaked. "Just shut up about it, will you?"

"Doug!" Sylvia snapped. "You don't have to be so obnoxious."

Better obnoxious than adorable, I thought.

The three of them went on with more talk about the wedding, but I tuned it all out. Instead, I focused my thoughts on Rudy and the good times we'd have for these next two weeks. Let the rest of them worry about the wedding. I was going to make the most of every minute with my goat.

My goat. When had I started thinking of Rudy as mine?

CHAPTER 8

This Goat's a Living Lawnmower

THE NEXT MORNING I overslept again. Everyone was finished eating when I got downstairs. In fact, only Sylvia and Missy were in the room. I wanted to rush down and check Rudy out right away. Woody had said he'd be over at the crack of dawn, but I was afraid to count on it.

"Doug, would you stop jiggling around?" Sylvia said. "Eat your breakfast. I have a lot to do this morning." She yelled toward the stairs, "Gloria, are you about ready?"

"Almost," Gloria called down.

"Don't worry about the dishes," Missy said. "We'll do them."

"All right. We're just going to dash to the bridal shop before Gloria goes to work. There's no need for you to go, Missy. They won't have a dress your size. I'll have to make it."

At last Gloria came down. "Let's go in your car, Sylvia. Greg will pick me up after work." They took off.

"I thought they'd never leave!" Missy said to me. "Quick, let's go down and see if Rudy's okay. I haven't heard a sound."

"Let's hope it's because Woody is there."

We rushed down the incline, and sure enough, Woody was on duty. So was Frank. They were standing to the side of the clubhouse, looking upward. Rudy was on the roof again.

"That dumb goat won't come down," Frank said. He gave the chain a savage yank. "Come on, stupid!"

"Don't do that, you creep!" I yelled. "You'll hurt him."

"Then *you* get him down, wise guy," Frank said.

Woody cleared his throat. He made a motion toward Missy. "I don't believe I've had the pleasure of . . ."

"Oh, Woody, this is Missy, my niece, the one I told you about."

Woody made a little bow. "It surely is a pleasure . . . Miss . . ."

"Just Missy. Are you new in the neighborhood?"

"Not really. But fairly new to the club, in which I have the honor of serving as president."

"Missy, this is Frank," I said with a scowl. "He's the new guy."

Frank gave her a glance, made a *huh* sound, and looked back at Rudy. "He's been up there a long time."

"Come on, baby," Missy coaxed, going closer to the shed. "Come down. We love you."

Rudy just looked at her in a pleasant sort of way.

"Come down, fella. Give yourself a break," Woody said. "No . . . scratch that *break* part. Don't break a leg. Or anything. Come down gently, gently."

"You coax him," Missy said to me. "He'll listen to you."

I decided to have a try. If all else failed, I could go get more carrots. Moving up close, I said softly, "Rudy, come down. I'm your friend, remember?"

Rudy gave me a long look, seemed to grin, and then jumped down gracefully to land beside me. It was almost embarrassing.

"You've really got the touch," Missy said with a bit of awe. *The boy who talks to goats.*

I shrugged. "He was ready to come down anyway." Inside, though, I felt really great. Rudy did seem to realize that we were friends.

"Have you fed him yet?" I asked, still petting Rudy.

Woody cleared his throat. "We . . . uh . . . thought we'd wait until the shed was . . . uh . . ."

Frank was more direct. "It's your turn to clean it out."

Oh, woooo. Big deal, I thought. When I stepped inside, though, I was nearly bowled over. All this smell from one goat?

"I'll help," Missy said, right behind me.

"You don't have to." I shook out a plastic bag and grabbed the shovel. That niece of mine took the bag and held it open and didn't even change expression. Even Frank looked impressed. He had probably thought she'd pass out.

As I slung the tied-up bag next to the others, Missy said, "Ask them about the rope, Doug. The rope to use instead of a chain."

"All right." I told Woody and Frank that the chain seemed awfully heavy for everyday use. "Why don't we try a rope? I think we have some. It used to be a clothesline before Mom got the dryer."

The guys said okay, so Missy and I ran off to get the rope from the basement while they stayed to watch Rudy.

Just as Missy and I came back upstairs, Sylvia suddenly appeared. "I forgot the grocery list," she said. "Now what are you two going to do with that rope?"

"Uh . . ." I stammered.

"If it's a mountain climbing game this time, forget it."

Missy and I chorused, "Nothing like that!"

"Then what? Are you planning to tie up someone?"

"Oh no," Missy said. "We wouldn't tie up any kid."

To myself, I said, *Not a kid. A full-grown goat, honk-honk.*

"All right. I know I can trust you," my sister said. She made it sound like a warning. Then she took off again, not noticing we hadn't done the dishes yet.

When we got back, Woody was holding onto the chain while Rudy happily grazed a little farther from the shed. "Look at that. He's cropped the grass and weeds in no time." Woody said. "This creature is a living lawnmower if I ever saw one."

As soon as we unclipped the chain from his collar

Rudy began frolicking around. He sure did have a lot of energy.

"Just see how happy he is," Missy said. "That proves the chain was too heavy for his sweet little neck. Isn't that right, Doug?"

At that moment, Rudy gave a spirited leap and took off along the path by the creek.

"Hey, stop!" we yelled as we took off after him.

Frank was fastest, then Missy. I came along next, and Woody puffed behind. With rocks here and there and tufts of grassy weeds jutting out from the creek bank, it was hard running. For us, that is. Rudy was sure-footed as anything. If he'd wanted to, he could have gotten away from us in a minute. He'd stop every now and then, though, and look back at us as though he were enjoying the chase. Finally he stopped altogether and waggled his chin back and forth until we reached him.

I took hold of his collar while we all caught our breath. We heard the tinkling of dog tags.

"Would you look at that!" Missy pointed to the way we'd come. "It's Prince, with the rope in his mouth!"

Sure enough, old Prince had taken hold of that clothesline and dragged it along while he chased after us. "Hey, Prince," I said. "You're not so dumb after all."

"Ssssh," Missy said.

"Oh, that mutt's too stupid to understand," Frank said. "Here, give me the rope, boy. That's a good dog-gie." He tied one end to Rudy's collar and looped the other and held on to it.

Woody, who was breathing normally by now, said, "As long as we're this far away, why don't we just cut through that vacant lot to the street and walk back on the sidewalk? It would be a lot easier. Also, we might flush out some business."

"What are you talking about?" I asked.

"You remember I said a while back that I had ideas for raking in some cash? With Rudy's help? So let's give it a try."

"What if someone from our families sees us?" I felt pretty nervous about showing Rudy off that way.

"My parents are away at a conference for the day," Woody said. "Your dad's at work, right, Frank? And your mother . . ." Woody glanced at his watch. "She'll be watching the soaps."

Frank nodded. "Every day, from ten-thirty until two."

Woody turned to me. "Your mom's out of town, Doug. Your dad's at the paper. And didn't you say the sisters were out shopping?"

"Yeah." Still, I felt uneasy. "Neighbors. Who's to say they wouldn't see us?"

"Look, there are four of us. It could be anyone's goat. Right?" Woody beamed. "So not to worry."

We made our way up the incline and walked across the vacant lot until we hit the sidewalk. "I wish you'd tell us exactly what you intend to do and say, Woody," I told him. I wanted to be prepared. My friend could get a little far out at times.

Just then we were passing in front of Mrs. Ida Cullerton's house. She was by the front steps, tying creeping roses onto a trellis. As she turned, she caught sight of us.

"Why, children, what have you got there?" she called out. She was a very friendly woman who passed out cookies to kids any time she saw them.

We headed up her front walk.

"We're baby-sitting a goat," I said. "Kid-sitting, I guess you'd call it." I knocked my elbow against Missy's and said "Honk honk."

"A goat. Well, if that isn't the nicest thing!" Ida Cullerton said, brushing a wisp of white hair out of her eyes. She petted Rudy on the head. "And so well behaved for an animal!"

Old jealous Prince rubbed against Mrs. Cullerton's legs and rolled his eyes and whimpered.

"And Prince," she said. She had to stoop over to pat him because he was now crawling on his stomach.

One way you can tell if grownups are really nice or not is if they remember the name of your dog. Ida knew every dog in the neighborhood, and a cat or two besides.

"And who is this young lady?" she asked. "Are you new in the neighborhood, dear?"

"This is my niece, Missy," I told Ida.

"Sylvia's girl! Well, I declare, you've just grown up nicer and prettier than a body could imagine."

"Thank you," Missy said. And then, "Those are certainly pretty roses."

"Well, yes, they are. But I'm just not up to gardening the way I used to be. I like caring for the flowers well enough, but keeping the yard . . . the grass . . ."

Woody cleared his throat, and I noticed his ears were starting to turn red. "Mrs. Cullerton," he said, "perhaps we could help you in that department." He cleared his throat again. "You see before you here a living lawn-mower." He pointed to Rudy. "This amiable creature could keep your grass cropped. I'm speaking purely as a favor — there'd be no charge for his services." By now Woody's ears were the color of fire.

"Goodness! What an interesting suggestion," Mrs. Cullerton said. "But wouldn't the poor thing get sick?"

"Oh no, ma'am," Frank said. "Goats can eat any-thing, almost."

Mrs. Cullerton looked a little dubious. "Well, if you're sure. I wouldn't mind getting that grass cut."

"And hauled away at the same time," Woody said. "Let's see if Rudy's interested." He motioned to Frank to play out the rope a bit. Rudy, with his little goat grin, walked over and started grazing.

"There's your demonstration," Woody said. "The best little lawnmower that money can buy."

After a while we left, promising Ida Cullerton we'd bring Rudy over soon. Each of us had a fistful of cook-ies she'd given us.

"I don't know why you had to be so fast to say there'd be no charge," Frank mumbled through a mouthful of peanut jumbles.

"One satisfied customer talks up your service,"

Woody said, "and before you know it, you're snowed under with requests. And don't forget, Ida Cullerton is someone special. I guess you could call her the neighborhood cookie connection."

We must have looked strange strolling down the street, the four of us, with Rudy trotting along, giving a bleat now and then between his share of cookies. Prince was frisking around, too, like a clown in a circus parade. Kids stopped playing to stare, and a couple of cars slowed down to give us a look.

As we got close to our house I started getting definitely nervous again. "Guys," I said, "We'd better cut back down to the creek. My sister may be home."

"If she's upstairs, looking out, she could have seen us already," Woody said. "Tell you what. Frank and I will take Rudy back and tie him up. You and Missy stroll on home, as though you were out for a walk and just happened to run into us." That Woody was always thinking.

The guys left, taking Rudy. Poor Prince didn't know which way he wanted to go, but I told him to come with us. After I dragged him for a few feet, he got my meaning.

When we were almost home, Missy remembered we hadn't done the dishes as promised. We dashed into the kitchen and put them into the dishwasher fast. I shook the crumbs from the placemats onto the floor while Missy sponged off the table.

Just then Sylvia came in. "Well," she said, looking

around, "everything's cleaned up. I thought you'd forget and go off somewhere. Next time I'll know I can trust you to follow through."

Missy and I didn't know what to say, so we didn't say anything.

CHAPTER 9

Rudy Gets Rainboots

ALL SYLVIA AND GLORIA did during dinner that night was yak about the wedding plans. Sylvia was really rolling. "You see, Gloria," she said, "there's a logical place to begin and then you progress, step by step, until the whole thing is under control."

Gloria looked a bit dazed. "That sounds good, but I just feel it's so hopeless." She sighed.

"It's not at all hopeless," Sylvia stated. "Gloria, the first thing you must do is make it clear to Alice and Tricia that adorable as those dresses may be, they just won't do for your wedding."

"But you didn't like the ones at the bridal shop either," Gloria pointed out.

Now Sylvia sighed. "I wish there was more time. You know what I'd really like to do? I'd like to hand-paint those bridsmaids' dresses."

"Really, Sylvia?" Gloria exclaimed.

"Maybe I could," Sylvia said thoughtfully. "Pick up some pastel voile, stitch up something simple, and paint on flowers."

"Hand-painted! Flowers! Oh, I can't wait to tell the girls," Gloria said, rising. "I'll call them right now!"

Sylvia took hold of her wrist and pulled her back down. "Don't say anything yet. There's no one at the design studio right now to ship me the paints, and I'm not sure I can find the right kind here. I just wish we had more than two weeks!"

"Postpone the wedding," Dad said. "Or Gloria, elope. That would be the best thing, I should think."

"Oh, Daddy! You're kidding." Gloria looked disturbed. "You *are* kidding, aren't you?"

"Of course he is," Sylvia said. "But let's talk about something else. Tell me, Dad, what's new and exciting in town? Any scandal? Any loonies running around?"

"Not at present," Dad said. "But stick around. They usually show up when there's a full moon."

Dad was just kidding again . . . I hoped.

It rained the next day and for several days after. Sylvia was in a bad mood. "With so much humidity in the air, there's no point in my even trying to paint that fabric," she said. "It'd never dry."

I was one hundred percent sick of that subject. "Why don't you buy those dumb bridesmaids' dresses at that dumb shop and get it over with?" I said. "No one's going to care anyway. It's just a wedding, not a Rose Bowl game or some other world event."

"Thank you for your frank opinion," Sylvia said.

She was just being sarcastic, but the next morning she said, "I've decided to run over to the bridal shop and go through the dresses again. Maybe I can find something that will do. Tell Gloria when she wakes up," she said to Missy. "I don't know how she can sleep in like this on her morning off."

"She stays out so late at night," Missy said.

Sylvia paused at the door. "What are you two going to do while I'm gone?"

"We'll maybe go outside and . . . uh . . ."

"In this rain?"

"It's only a drizzle," I said, looking out the window. "Anyway, it's dry in the clubhouse. I'll probably go down and clean it up."

Sylvia looked a bit suspicious. "Just don't track a lot of mud into the house," she said.

"Okay, okay."

As soon as she had gone, Missy and I streaked down to the clubhouse. I hadn't lied. It *was* my day to clean.

"Oh, poor Rudy," Missy crooned as he stood looking forlorn in the doorway of the shed. "You haven't been able to run around for ages."

Prince ran inside the shed and frisked around Rudy.

"Get out," I told him. "It doesn't matter if *your* feet get wet."

"I wish there was some way . . ." Missy said as we worked around Rudy, shoveling the stuff from the floor into a bag. "Oh, Doug! I have an idea! Why don't we make rainboots for Rudy?"

I straightened and looked at her. "How would we do that?"

"Cut them out of plastic and tie them on. We could do it, Doug!"

It sounded okay to me. "You mean like that plastic wrap for food?"

"No, heavier. I know! We could cut some pieces from that heavy plastic cover over the feed outside. Just some from the edge. Shall I run up and get scissors? And something for ties?"

"Sure. Maybe rubber bands. Hey, Prince, get out of my way." He lit out after Missy.

She came back in a little bit. "Here are the scissors, and some ribbon Aunt Gloria found for me. She's just getting up."

"*Pink* ribbon?"

"It's all she had. It doesn't matter, Doug. I think goats are color-blind anyway. Most animals are, you know." Missy put fodder into the feeder for Rudy. "Aunt Gloria didn't even ask why I wanted the ribbon. She's so good-natured."

"She sure is, even half-asleep." I went out and cut out four squares of plastic, dried one side off on my pants, and took them inside. Together, Missy and I wrapped them up around Rudy's hooves and tied them on. "Not too tight," Missy warned. "We don't want to cut off his circulation. Oh Prince, please get out of the way!"

"Beat it, bird-brain," I told the dog.

"I do believe he wants rainboots, too," Missy said, leaning back on her heels. "Shall we make some for him?"

"Why bother? His feet are already wet. Come on, Rudy, you can go outside now."

That goat acted as though he'd been released from prison. We let him frolic around for a while and then tied him to the stake. Suddenly Missy stiffened. "Did you hear my mother call just now?"

"No."

"I think I did. I'll run up so she doesn't come down to get us."

"I'll come along, too. I'm hungry. Let's leave the clubhouse door open so Rudy can get back inside if it starts to rain hard again."

At the house we took off our shoes and left them at the back door.

"It's too bad Prince didn't have shoes to take off," Sylvia said by way of greeting. "Look how he's muddied up the floor. Out, Prince!" She pushed him outside, and we walked on into the kitchen.

"I ordered the dresses," Sylvia was saying to Gloria, who was up now and dressed and drinking coffee. "I can still paint the flowers on them if things work out. Are you about ready? We'd better get a move on if you have a two o'clock permanent to do." To us, she said, "You kids might as well come along. We're going over to Mrs. Langley's house to select the wedding cake."

"You mean she has cakes sitting around all the time?" I asked. I hoped Mrs. Langley might pass out free samples.

Gloria laughed. "Honey, she just has pictures of them."

"Pictures? You're not going to have just a *picture* of a cake, are you?"

I really was confused, but Sylvia said, "Stop trying to be funny, Doug, and go get a raincoat. You, too, Missy. It might start pouring again."

I thought Mrs. Langley might live in a gingerbread-looking house, but it was just an ordinary split-level. She got up from watching a soap opera to greet us.

"Well, Gloria," Mrs. Langley said, "I'm as pleased as anything to be making your wedding cake. You'll be a beautiful bride."

"Oh, thank you!" Gloria said breathlessly. You'd think she'd never been told before that she was beautiful. "Oh, do you know my sister, Sylvia Sherman? And my niece, Melissa?"

There was the usual "nice to meet you" baloney, and then Mrs. Langley said, "And is this Douglas? Why, the last time I remember seeing you, you were in diapers. How time flies!"

I wished I could fly right out of the window. Missy acted as though she hadn't heard, though. Thank goodness Frank wasn't around.

Mrs. Langley brought out the photos in a loose-leaf notebook. She took out the pages and passed them around as we sat at the dining room table.

"Oh, yummy!" Missy said upon seeing each of them. I was almost drooling myself. I mean, those cakes towered in the air and were just loaded with icing in all kinds of designs.

"Oh, I can't decide," Gloria said after we'd seen

about twelve or fifteen photos. "What do you think, Mrs. Langley?"

"It's to be a small wedding, I understand. In the garden?"

"If it doesn't rain," Missy said. Her mother gave her a dirty look.

"How many guests would you say?"

"Ummm." Gloria wrinkled her pretty brow. "Our family is four . . . no, six with Missy and Sylvia. And the aunts, that's three, and two of their husbands, Aunt Gracie's left her, and let's see, my friends Terry and . . ."

Sylvia said firmly, "Count on thirty."

"Thirty." Mrs. Langley shuffled through the photos and picked out three. "These are your best bets. I can add or take away a layer on any of them. They turn out real nice every time."

"So Gloria, choose," Sylvia said.

"Oh." Gloria sighed over each of them. "They're all so yummy-looking." She bit her lips, then looked up. "Missy, you choose. After all, as junior bridesmaid, you should know what's best."

"Really?" Missy beamed. She studied each photo and held out the one with swoops of icing running up and down and pink roses all over the place. "This one."

Mrs. Langley beamed. "That's a wonderful design. Actually, my favorite. Now, Gloria, do you want the traditional white cake?"

"I hate white cake," Gloria said. "It tastes so . . . vanilla."

"So do I," I said, though no one had asked my opinion. "Gloria, how about devil's food?"

"Devil's food? For a wedding?" Sylvia exclaimed.

"All right, then strawberry," Gloria said.

"Strawberry shortcake, mmmm," Missy said.

Mrs. Langley broke in. "How about a white cake with strawberry flavoring? It could have pink running through it, and that would go real well with the pink rose decorations."

They went on to discuss sizes and what date and time the cake would be delivered. Missy and I slipped off to watch the soap opera. It was just getting good, with some guy telling his girlfriend she was a tramp, when we had to leave.

We all had lunch at a place with a salad bar, and then we dropped Gloria off at the beauty shop.

"When I was a little kid," Missy said, "I used to think Aunt Gloria was so beautiful because she was always at the beauty shop. Why are we stopping here at this store?" she asked her mother.

"I want to run in and get some fabric. This afternoon I'll see if the new paints I bought will be okay. If they don't work out, that's that. We'll just go with the plain dresses."

"Could we take in a movie, Missy and me?" I asked. "So we won't get in your way?"

My sister looked as though she liked the idea, but then she had to add, "You may, if there's something decent to see."

She got out of the car, put up her umbrella, and almost bumped into a man who was hurrying by. She

78

stopped to apologize, I guess, and he must have been someone she knew, because she broke out in a big smile and shook hands with him. They stood there, looking happy, talking away, until finally Sylvia left to go into the store.

When she got back, she began talking about the fabric she'd found, but Missy interrupted with "Who was that man?"

"Man?" Sylvia started the car. "Oh, you mean the one I was talking with? That's Larry Williams. I used to know him . . . oh, way back when."

"Was he your boyfriend?" Missy asked.

"Boyfriend?" Sylvia braked for a car that backed out ahead of us. "I guess you could say . . . well . . . we went out together."

"How long?"

"How long?" We took off down the street. "How long did we go out together? A couple of years. Three maybe. That was ages ago."

"How come you didn't marry him?" Boy, that Missy could really zero in when she felt like it.

"Sweetie, you don't marry every guy you go out with."

"Debbie's mother does. She's been married four times."

"Missy, I don't know if you're trying to be funny or annoying, but I don't appreciate it, so cut it out."

We pulled up in front of the theatre. "Good," Sylvia said, "that horse movie is on." She reached into her purse. "Here's the money. There's enough for popcorn, too. If it's raining afterward, call and I'll come for you. Otherwise, I guess you can manage to walk the few blocks."

When we were inside the lobby, Missy said, "She still likes that Williams guy."

"How can you tell?"

"He put her in a good mood. She doesn't usually let me buy popcorn."

I hadn't thought Sylvia's mood was all that great, but I guess Missy knows her mother better than I do.

The sky was clearing up when we got out of the movie. It felt good to walk after several days of being cooped up. By the time we got home, the sun was shining.

My big sister, too, seemed unusually sunny. "How was the flick?" she asked, blotting her shampooed hair with a towel.

"Oh, good," Missy said. "But sad, when they took the horse away. He got to come back home, though."

"Wonderful," Sylvia said. She said it in the way adults do when they're not really listening. "I'm going to sit on the back steps. I love to dry my hair in the sun. Keep me company?"

"Okay," Missy said.

I had nothing better to do, so I went out with them.

"Oh, Prince, Prince, get away," Missy said as the dog tried to climb into her lap. "Sit here and I'll pet you. Nice doggie."

"Prince sure does love Missy," I commented.

"All animals do." Sylvia draped an arm around her daughter. "She has such a sweet, loving nature."

"I wish I could have a dog," Missy said.

"I do too, honey, but you know we can't in our apartment."

"When we move, then? You *said* when we move."

"I said 'maybe.' It depends on *where*."

"But you said we'd move someplace that . . ."

"Missy, please." Sylvia began lifting her long hair and letting it fall. "Oh, by the way, you guys are going to be on your own this evening until Dad — Grandpa — gets home. He has a short staff meeting, but he'll be along later."

"Why? Where will you be?" Missy asked her mother.

"Ummm . . . Larry — Mr. Williams — asked me out to dinner tonight. To talk over old times."

"Alone?"

Sylvia laughed. "Are you suggesting we need a chaperone?"

Missy scowled. "What about his wife?"

"He's divorced." Sylvia stood up. "Anyway, chickie, it's just old friends renewing . . . friendship. What would you like for dinner?"

Missy didn't answer, so I said, "Hamburgers."

"Oh, poor Dad." Sylvia stood up. "I've got to do my nails. I should have gone to the beauty shop and let Gloria do them."

After she left, I said to Missy, "Want to go down and play with Rudy for a while?"

"No, you go. I don't feel like it."

I got up and started to say, "Sure you do," but something in Missy's expression kept me from it. Poor kid. She was sitting there with her lips pressed together as though she didn't trust herself to say anything else.

When I turned to go, Prince started to follow, but then he stopped, looked back at Missy and then at me. "Go stay with her, boy," I said. "Be nice to Missy."

For once he obeyed my orders. But then I always had the feeling he loved my niece more than he loved me.

I felt sorry for Missy just sitting there alone, except for Prince. Why was she feeling so down, just because her mother was going out with some guy? It didn't seem all that big a deal to me.

Rudy was really glad to see me. I checked his boots. One ribbon had worked loose, so I retied it. Although the sun was out full force now, it was still damp down by the creek.

"Tomorrow, buddy, I'll turn you loose for a while," I said to him. "You'll like that, won't you, Rudy?"

He nuzzled against my chest. Little did I suspect that Rudy had no intention of waiting until tomorrow.

CHAPTER 10

Just a Hillbilly Goat

THE NEXT MORNING when I went down to break-fast, everyone was in the kitchen except Sylvia. The first thing that came to my mind was, *She's run off with that guy*!

Missy looked okay, though, sitting there reading the comics. "Where's your mom?" I asked as I sat down and poured my cereal.

"She went to drop off some things at the cleaners. She'll be right back," Missy said.

Dad glanced up at the clock. "Your aunt Harriet's surgery was early this morning. We're waiting for a call. I hope everything went all right."

"Poor Auntie," Gloria said with a sigh. "All this suffering, and not being able to come to the wedding."

Sylvia came in just as the phone rang. She walked over to answer. "Yes, just a minute," she said. She turned to Dad, "It's for you. The paper, I think."

"Thanks." Dad took the phone. Sylvia and Gloria were saying something but stopped at the sound of Dad's voice. "They *what*? Will you repeat that, Scotty?" Pause. "My word, and there's not even a full moon."

We all exchanged looks.

Dad went on, "No, I don't want you to write it up. Check it out. Get names, and details. I'll be there in a little while, Scotty. All right. Thanks."

He hung up and stood there shaking his head.

"What's going on?" Sylvia asked.

Dad gave a bewildered little laugh. "Someone called in to say a nut was on the loose last night."

"A loony?" Missy gasped.

Dad put his cup and saucer in the sink. "Most likely the loony is whoever it was who called in. Get this: They claim they saw someone with white hair. Not blond. White. Looking in their window. When they went outside they saw the bushes had been trampled. And the ground was still soft enough to show footprints. *Round* footprints."

"Round?" Sylvia looked baffled. "What kind of shoes would leave round footprints?"

"And another thing. They found a pink ribbon. Does any of that make a bit of sense?"

To me it did. I gave Missy a quick look. From her wide-eyed expression I could tell she was thinking the same thing I was. White hair. Round footprints. Pink ribbon. It all added up to . . . Rudy!

A glance at Gloria showed that the pink ribbon thing hadn't registered.

Getting up, I tripped over my own feet. "I'm going

84

down to see if he . . . the guys, I mean . . . are at the clubhouse," I said. No one seemed to care except Missy. I put a hand to my ear and glanced at Dad. She nodded to show she understood: *Stay and listen for any other news.*

I rushed down toward the shed, not knowing what would be there. Rudy was, grazing contentedly. When he spied me, he gave a little leap and trotted over.

"Hey, fella, have you been up to something?" I asked. A quick check showed that indeed he had been. The rainboot on his right rear hoof was missing. "Don't you know you could get yourself and us, too, in a lot of trouble?" I asked. "Now, hold still. I've got to get these other three boots off you." I managed to untie the ribbons, even though they were muddy and knotted, and started to stick them in my pocket. But . . . *Get rid of the evidence*, the detective part of my brain said. I put the ribbons and the boots into one of the garbage bags with the messed-up peanut shells. No one in his right mind would sift through that stuff.

"Doug!" I heard Missy calling. She came into sight. "Was it . . . ?" She looked at Rudy.

"It sure was. One of the rainboots was missing."

"Wow. What a close call!"

I had calmed down a lot. "Not so close. No one even suspected it was a goat."

"No, I mean that we didn't make those plastic boots for Prince, too, with the pink ribbons."

I blew out my breath. "My gosh. That was a close one." I fastened the end of the rope back to the stake. "Did Dad get any more calls or anything?"

"From Grandma. Oh . . . I forgot. That's why they sent me down to get you. So you can talk to her. Aunt Harriet's okay."

"Good." I tested Rudy's rope. It seemed to hold. "You be good now," I said to Rudy just before leaving. "I don't want to hear a sound out of you." We were really lucky that Rudy, except for right at first when he felt strange, didn't *maaa-aaa* very often. He seemed to be pretty well adjusted for a goat.

As we climbed back up to the house I said, "I wish everyone would get off the phone and go somewhere else. Woody is supposed to call and let me know what time he and Frank are coming over. We're taking Rudy around today. To sign him up for lawn work."

"What about that nice lady with the roses?"

"Mrs. Cullerton? We'll do her yard later. We've got to get Rudy booked up, Woody says, because we just have next week, and then he'll be gone."

"Oh, that makes me so sad. I wish Rudy could be yours forever, Doug."

I didn't answer. I couldn't. I wasn't even letting myself think about Rudy going back to Oliver's.

When we walked into the kitchen I saw that Gloria and Dad had gone. Sylvia was talking on the phone. "Oh, here are the kids," she said. "Doug, Mother wants to talk to you."

"Hey, Mom," I said. "I guess you're feeling relieved. We were afraid Aunt Harriet was going to die right there on the operating table."

I thought that was a nice thing to say, but Sylvia hissed, "Doug!"

I turned my back on her. "What was that you said, Mom?" I asked.

"I said our prayers were answered," she said.

"For sure. How soon are you coming back?"

"Honey, I don't know. As soon as your aunt is out of danger."

"Will you be back in time to see . . ." Oh no! I'd almost said *to see Rudy before he leaves.*

"To see Gloria married? Of course I will. I'll be there in a few days, I hope. Sylvia tells me everything is under control there and that you and Missy have been behaving like angels."

I doubted that my sister had said those exact words. "Well, we're keeping busy . . . with this and that."

"Good. I certainly do miss you, honey."

"I miss you, too, Mom." Right at that moment I really wanted my mom to be there, putting her arms around me and bending her face down to kiss my forehead the way she sometimes did. But I couldn't say so. Anyway, Missy was jiggling around, waiting for her turn to talk. "Here's your favorite granddaughter," I said. I'd have to stop that little joke if Gloria ever had a girl baby.

After Missy was finished, Sylvia got back on and started talking about guess what, the wedding. "Oh yes, Mother, they promised the dresses would definitely be here in time." She gave a little laugh. "I'm sorry I ever mentioned painting flowers on those gowns, but I'll have a try at it. I'm going to test it on just plain fabric first." She paused. "No, I have to make Missy's. It will be simple." There was a longer pause and then she said, "No, Mother, I don't mind. Really. It's best to get these little things taken care of before the grand rush."

When she hung up I found out what one of the little things was that she was taking care of. Buying me a pair of shoes.

"Why do I need shoes?" I asked, holding up my sneakered foot. "I got these just two months ago."

"You know very well, Doug, that you can't wear those to a wedding. You're to get a sport jacket, too. And Missy needs shoes."

"Oh goody," my niece said. "Can I get some silver ones with high heels and ankle straps? For my bridesmaid outfit?"

Sylvia eyed her daughter. "You're to be in a wedding, not a chorus line. Honestly. You kids." She left the room, telling us we were leaving in a few minutes and to wash and put on clean socks.

I got on the phone with Woody. "What's keeping you guys?" I asked.

"We're about to leave," he said. "Are you ready?"

"Something's come up," I said. I hated to admit I had to do a silly thing like shopping, but there was no help for it.

Woody understood. "No problem, old sport," he said. "First things first. In this case, family."

"Yeah. Listen, Woody, I have to talk to you guys about something important."

"Shoot."

"I can't over the telephone. Could we schedule a meeting later today? Say around three?"

"Of course. I'll give Frank the word."

"See you then. I've got to scram now." I went upstairs. Sylvia was just coming out of her room. "Aren't you ready yet, Doug? Get a move on. I've lots of things to do today."

The phone rang. Oh gosh. "I'll get it!" I yelled, spinning toward the stairs.

"No, just go and get ready," Sylvia said impatiently. "I'll take the call in the folks' room."

Hoping it wasn't Woody calling back, I went off to change my socks. I was just tying the shoelaces when Missy came to my door. "It's him," she half-whispered. "On the phone, talking to Mother."

"Oh, no! Can you tell what Woody's saying?"

"Not Woody. *Him*. That Larry guy."

Oh, so what, I thought. Who cared? I got up to go. Missy was standing there, looking uneasy.

"Want to go downstairs and listen in?" I asked her.

"Oh, I couldn't!"

"I guess not. Let's go stand in the doorway, though, to make her nervous."

Missy was a little scared to, but I wasn't. After all, it was my house.

I stood in the doorway. Sylvia looked up. I really wished I had a wristwatch so I could tap it the way I'd seen a guy do on TV to let his wife know it was time to leave the party.

"Just a minute, Larry," Sylvia said. Then, holding her hand over the mouthpiece, she said, "You kids go get in the car. I'll be right there."

I could tell Missy was in a troubled mood because

she didn't talk in the car. Even when she tried on four pairs of white shoes at the store and got to take her choice, she wasn't exactly bubbling over with joy.

Sylvia pretended not to notice, but I caught her giving Missy a serious look. At that moment I felt a little sorry for my sister. She had a great job at that design studio and she had Missy, but she probably got lonesome at times. That would explain why Larry was a big deal to her just now.

"Hey, that pair is the greatest!" I said about the shoes Missy finally chose. "They make your feet look real little, like the ones the runner-up in the Miss Universe contest was wearing on TV the other night."

Normally, my sister would have said to me, "Doug, what rubbish!" But seeing Missy smile, she smiled, too.

After I got my shoes, we broke for lunch. That was fine, but then the afternoon dragged on and on. We went to about a million places so I could try on sports jackets and slacks. Then Sylvia insisted I wear a regular shirt and tie with the outfit we finally bought. The clerk, who had seemed okay up to now, sided with Sylvia. "Sorry, fella," he said, "but even if your Save the Whales T-shirt *is* white, it just won't do for a wedding."

I was beginning to get a little nervous. It was after two o'clock. What if the guys tethered Rudy and he got loose again? I had to get back and warn them, so I didn't put up any more arguments about the clothes. Sylvia looked pleased with our purchases and said the folks would be proud of me.

They wouldn't be so proud, I thought, if our goat went on a rampage and really destroyed things. We could even be sued, probably, and taken for everything we owned.

I was really jittery by the time we got home.

"Now where do you two think you're going?" my sister asked, as Missy and I threw our packages on the kitchen table and dashed toward the door.

"Just down to the clubhouse. We have a meeting, and I'm late," I said.

"Missy, you're not going," Sylvia said. "I've got to start on your dress right away, and I need you here so I can take measurements."

Poor Missy was eager to have her bridesmaid dress made, but she was also anxious about Rudy.

"I'll keep you posted," I told her.

"I can still remember our get-togethers down at the clubhouse," Sylvia said with a little smile. "We used to think they were so important!" She gave me a pat on the back of my head. "Run along. If any earth-shaking news develops, there's still time to get it in the paper."

She was joking, but her words made my blood run cold.

The guys were just tying up Rudy when I got there.

"Well, Doug," Woody said, "how was shopping? What color scheme are you going with for the wedding?"

"Never mind about that," I said. "I have to tell you guys something superserious." I reminded them about the boots and ribbons we'd made for Rudy, and then laid on the news about the call that came into the paper. It put the guys into a state of shock, as I knew it would.

"If he can work that rope loose, we'll just have to

put the chain back on Rudy," Frank said. "Much as we hate to do it."

Woody cleared his throat. "I anticipate a continued problem," he said. "I hate to put a damper on things, but it occurs to me that Rudy is quite restless."

"So what else is new?" I asked.

"Remember, the rain kept him a prisoner for several days. Then last night he managed to get loose, and tore around town. Now today, he went out, to be sure, but on a short leash. And now we tie him up again."

"Would you come to the point?" Frank said with a scowl.

"I imagine Rudy is looking forward to another spree tonight." He held up a hand as Frank started to interrupt. "He won't be able to run, of course, because of the chain. So what will he do? He'll bellow. Like he's never bellowed before. The whole neighborhood will hear him."

Woody shook his head. "It will all be over, men. And just when we were about to strike the mother lode."

"The *who*?" I asked.

"Meaning, we were all set to clean up. Make money. We had four possibles today, didn't we, Frank? Four women who said if Rudy works out for Mrs. Ida Cullerton, they'd think of hiring him."

"Forget about making money right now, will you, Woody?" I said. "What we have to do is think of some way to keep Rudy quiet tonight. What'll we do? Take turns sleeping in the shed with him?"

Woody made a little face. I didn't blame him. Even if we put clean carpet inside the clubhouse, it still wouldn't be a place you'd want to spend the night.

As I looked at Woody, his expression slowly changed until he was actually beaming. "I've got it!" he said with a snap of his fingers.

"What?"

"Remember when they brought Rudy over in the truck, and Oliver was riding in the back with him?"

"Yeah. So?"

"Remember what Oliver said?" Neither Frank nor I did. "He said, 'Rudy likes country-western music'!"

The light dawned. "Yeah!" I said. "So we get a radio and tune it to country-western. Right? For Rudy to listen to all night?"

"You've got the idea. Only . . ." Woody frowned. "There's no outlet to plug the radio into."

"Maybe we could get a bunch of extension cords and run them down from your house, Doug," Frank said.

"Too tricky," I said. "We'll have to get a radio that runs on batteries. Our family doesn't have any. Do you guys?"

They shook their heads no. Then Woody brightened and snapped his fingers again. "I've got it! My Walkman! It runs on batteries! Guys, how about this? We could put the earphones on Rudy and strap the tape deck to his middle. There'll be that music running into his head and blowing out all thought of running away. It'll work! I know it'll work!"

I had to hand it to Woody. He might be a little weird at times, but in a crisis he always came through.

The two of them went off to get the stuff. I said I'd stay with Rudy so he could have a little freedom. He didn't need a tether as long as someone was with him.

I watched him sniff and munch here and there. I couldn't help but think how great it would be if he were mine for keeps and didn't need to be kept a secret anymore. We'd have such good times together.

As though he could read my mind, Rudy came over, sniffed my arm, and then sank gracefully to the ground beside me. He was friendly with everyone. But did I imagine it, or did he really have a special affection for me? I know I felt closer to him than any animal I'd ever been around.

As I was thinking this, Rudy put his face right next to mine and nuzzled my cheek. "You really belong to me, don't you?" I whispered.

He gave the slightest little sound and put his head on my knee. I was glad no one was around to see the moisture in my eyes.

CHAPTER 11

Rudy Goes to Work

I WAS DOWN THERE for about an hour with my goat. That's how I thought of Rudy when there was no one else around. As mine. I just wouldn't let myself think of the days passing by, each one coming closer to the time when he'd be taken away.

When I talked to him, he'd bend his head a little to the side as though taking it all in. They say dolphins can understand human talk. I swear Rudy could understand mine. "It seems so peaceful," I told him, "just to be here talking to you." As it turned out, it was the last peaceful hour either of us would have for some time.

Missy kept racing down to visit. She was dying to hang around so she could see Rudy's reaction when Woody and Frank brought the Walkman. She couldn't stay, though. "Mom's really sewing up a storm," she told me. "It doesn't take her long to whip a dress together. I've got to go back, in case she needs to fit or measure some more."

Finally the guys arrived, looking triumphant. "Well, Doug," Woody said, "here's our solution." He held up a Walkman, with earphones dangling. "I brought along a luggage strap, to hold it onto Rudy," he said. "Frank, keep it in place up here on his back, and I'll fasten the strap around his middle."

"Did you get the country-western tape?" I asked.

"Sure did. I don't relate to that type of music myself, but I traded off with a guy I know. My stamps for his tape. Jim says it has some great numbers on it."

I knelt next to Rudy so I could put the earphones in my ears, and reached up to turn on the tape. Some guy was singing *"Mamas, Don't Let Your Babies Grow Up to Be Cowboys."*

"That sure is western," I said, taking off the earphones and putting them on Rudy. He lifted his head, listened, and gave his best goat grin. "Hey, guys, look at that pleased expression," I said. "I wouldn't be surprised if this is his favorite song."

"Could be," Frank said. "Old Rudy's practically dancing. If he likes the other numbers as well, we're in business."

We hung around for quite a while, to let the tape run out. Then we rewound it, with the "Mamas" number all ready to roll.

"We might as well leave the earphones and tape in place," Woody said, "since Rudy doesn't seem to mind. One of us will have to come down tonight and turn on the tape. It's my belief that by the time it's finished playing, Rudy will be ready to go beddy-bye."

"Let's hope," I said. I was right in the thick of it, what with Rudy being close to my house and Dad so close to the newspaper reporters, and the police too, for that matter. I tried to brush away those worries. "I'll come down to turn on the tape," I told them. "And I'm going to put Rudy inside tonight and lock the shed. Just in case."

"He can't possibly get loose from that chain," Frank said. "But all the same, it'll be safer if you lock him up, too."

Gloria and Sylvia and even Missy were going to a bridal shower that night. Greg stopped by to have dinner with us, since he wouldn't be able to see Gloria for part of the evening. I couldn't understand that at all. Gloria's okay, but I could do without seeing her for a week or even a month. I guess Greg, who had been big in school sports, considered Gloria his personal cheerleader. They sure did get along together.

Missy was all excited about going to the party. "Why do they call it a shower, Aunt Gloria?" she asked.

"Because the guests shower the bride-to-be with gifts," my sister explained.

"They do? What kind of gifts?" Missy's eyes were bright with interest. "Rings and watches and makeup sets?"

"I don't think they give rings," Gloria said. "Or watches. It's more like toasters, towels, things for around the house."

Sylvia said, "Don't you remember, we got the —"

and she whispered in Missy's ear. "That's for tonight."

"Oh, I remember!"

Greg turned to me. "Hey, Doug, since the girls are going to be busy tonight, how about you keeping me company? Want to go bowling?"

"Sure!" I looked around. No one seemed to mind.

Later, as the three of them were about to leave, Gloria kissed Greg and then said to me, "Keep your eye on him for me, Doug. See that he doesn't make any passes at other women."

"Not a chance," Greg said. "I can't see other gals even when they're in plain sight."

If you didn't count mush stuff like that, Greg was a pretty good guy. He sure knew how to bowl. He didn't show off, though, or even laugh when one of my balls rolled down the gutter.

After a couple of games, Greg went to the refreshment stand and brought back a Coke for me and beer for himself. Along with the sound of pins falling and the machines setting new ones in place, there was the twang of country-western music coming from speakers. It reminded me of Rudy. Woody had said, sure, he'd start the tape, when I'd made that hurry-up call before Greg and I left. And he'd promised to lock Rudy up, too. I knew Woody could be trusted, but still I couldn't help but worry a little.

"Hey, Doug, what's the matter?" Greg grinned at me. "You look as though you're about to lose your best pal."

"I am, Greg." Rudy was my best pal, in a way. There'd never be another like him, either.

Greg put a hand onto my shoulder. "Listen, it's not as bad as all that. It may not be the same house, but it's the same town. You'll see her often."

"*Her*? Who?"

"Why, Gloria."

"Gloria? Ohhhhh . . . Gloria." Wow. What a close call. How could I explain? I couldn't. Instead, I said in a pathetic voice, "Greg, I'd rather not talk about it."

"Sure, I understand." He started to take another swallow of his beer, but instead he held out the can to me. "Take a swig, pal. You're the closest thing I have to a drinking buddy right now. Bottoms up!"

"Yeah?" I felt good about that. A drinking buddy, eh? I took a mouthful of beer, choked, and almost spit it out. I managed to swallow it, though. "I guess I'm not much of a drinker," I told Greg, handing it back.

"Hey, Doug, you're all right." He got up. "Let's have another game and then head back, okay?"

We played another. I got a strike. On the way home we stopped for some tacos, though I wasn't very hungry.

By the time we got back to the house, the others had returned. "Oh, Greg, honey, just wait until you see the loot!" Gloria said, all excited. "It's wonderful!"

"You guys got three toasters and a waffle iron!" Missy said. "And towels, and trays, and the cutest little cat clock! Its tail wags back and forth."

"What will they think of next?" Greg said, smiling and pulling Gloria to him.

"You kids get upstairs and to bed," Sylvia said. "Missy!" She took her daughter by the shoulders, turned her around, and pointed her toward the stairs.

"Good night," Missy and I called out.

Gloria and Greg stopped kissing long enough to wish us good night. "Don't forget now, Doug. We're buddies," Greg called out to me with a wink.

"Why are you buddies?" Missy asked as we went up the stairs.

"Because we had a drink together," I said. And at her shocked look, "Just a sip. Don't go making anything of it." I looked around to see if Sylvia was within earshot. She wasn't. I could hear the three of them down in the living room, laughing. "I'm going to duck into Dad's room and call Woody," I said. "To make sure he checked out Rudy."

I opened the door to my folks' room. Dad was in bed, reading. "What is it, Doug?"

"Oh. Just good night."

"Good night."

I closed the door and made a face.

"You can count on Woody," Missy said. "If he said he'd do it, he did."

"I guess you're right." I went to my window and listened; there wasn't a sound. I fell asleep fairly fast, but I had wild dreams all night long.

When the phone rang the next morning, I just knew it was the paper. It was.

"Hey, calm down, Scotty," Dad said, looking more than a bit upset himself. "Now, give me the facts one by one. You were where? At the office, writing a sports article. And this party called." Pause. "A wild creature, eh? Wearing *what*?" We could hear Scotty's voice, but couldn't make out the words. Dad said, "That's what they told you? And you actually believed it?"

"What . . . what . . . ?" Sylvia asked. "What's going on?"

"Hold on a minute, Scotty," Dad said. He turned to Sylvia and said, "Someone reported a wild creature was streaking through town last night with something fastened to its back, and dangling wires. So Scotty assumed the animal was set up with a bomb and sent out on some self-destruct mission."

"That's preposterous," Sylvia said.

"I know." Dad turned back to the phone. "Well, Scotty, have there been any reports of a bomb going off around town? What? What's that?" Pause.

I started shaking. I didn't dare look at Missy. I could feel her big round eyes fixed on me, though.

Dad was nodding, but his look shifted to Sylvia and he made the "he's crazy" kind of circle with his finger. "Now, let me get this straight, Scotty. You went out . . . caught sight of the creature yourself. And then you could see the wires were from a . . . *what*? What's a Walkman?" Pause. "I see."

I wanted to fade away. My heart was pounding.

"And what did you do next? Call the police and ask them to catch this wild creature and place it in custody? No? Well, that was a wise move, Scotty. They might not have believed you, I agree. The police are funny that way. Tell you what. Stay put. Don't talk to anyone about this. We don't want the TV stations to get hold of it and break the story ahead of us. We'll try to solve it first, and then we'll notify them. Right, Scotty. Don't leave. I'll be right there."

Dad hung up. "Good Lord, Scotty's off again. I thought the man had licked his drinking problem. I may have to let him go if he's hitting the booze like that."

"Fire him?" My voice sounded shrill. I lowered it. "You wouldn't want to fire Scotty just because he thought he saw a go — . . . a creature!"

Sylvia gave me a sharp look.

Good-hearted Missy added, "Grandpa, if someone else saw it . . . and called Scotty . . ."

Dad picked up his briefcase. "Scotty may have imagined that, too. People get all kinds of fantasies when they're under the influence of alcohol. Let that be a lesson to you, Doug. Don't ever start drinking." He left.

The second he was gone, Sylvia turned to me. "Doug, there's something on your mind, I can tell. What were you about to say to Dad? Let's hear it!"

For a second I stammered, and then I had a thought. "I was going to confess to him, but I didn't want to upset him more."

"Confess to what?"

"Drinking. I did take a sip of beer last night. When I was with Greg, at the bowling alley."

"Beer? A sip of beer?"

"Yes." In my most innocent way, I said, "Do you think that means I'll end up in Alcoholics Anonymous?"

I could tell it was all my sister could do to keep from

laughing, but she got up and managed to say, "I don't think one sip of beer is going to turn you into a hopeless drunk, Doug. But just don't do it again." She began picking up the breakfast dishes and told Missy and me to clear out.

We did, and headed straight for the clubhouse.

Rudy was there. The luggage strap had slipped and the Walkman was dangling pretty close to his front hooves. I took it all off.

"Rudy, Rudy, you were a holy terror, weren't you?" I leaned down and put my head next to his. "You upset all kinds of people. Even me."

Rudy turned his head and nibbled at my cheek.

"Poor thing, you just wanted to frolic, didn't you?" Missy said. "You got tired of being shut up in this old shed with no view."

"*Shut up in the shed*," I said straightening up. "He couldn't have been. He can't open the lock. Hey, his collar isn't even fastened to the chain. That Woody! Wait till I get hold of him!" Asking Missy to stay there with Rudy, I raced up to the house and phoned Woody to come over on the double, and bring Frank. Emergency meeting.

As soon as the guys showed up, I told them what had happened. Woody was full of apologies. "I came over and set up the tape," he said. "Rudy looked so happy I couldn't help but stand there and watch and laugh. Then I remembered a call I had to make to some guy about a rare stamp, and . . ."

"And you took off, just like that," I said. "So now we're in a lot of trouble, just because you didn't follow through. Do you know they may print the whole story in the paper, if my dad ends up believing Scotty? Where will we be then, I'd like to know!"

"Oh, relax," Frank said. "Your father's not going to believe that guy. And even if he does, so what? It could have been some other goat, you know. We don't even know for sure it *was* Rudy they saw!"

"Frank, you idiot. How many goats go trotting around with Walkmans strapped to their middles? In the dead of night!"

We heard Sylvia call for Missy. "Be right back," Missy said, taking off.

"Now, men," Woody said. "Let's not panic. The word *goat* has not been mentioned so far, and that's all to the good. Remember, we have only a few more days to keep Rudy, which means a short time to earn back some of our money. The rest we'll add up to entertainment."

"Do you mean to tell me," I asked, "that you're still thinking of taking Rudy out for lawn jobs? After all that's happened?"

"I told you. No one has made the connection, and they won't, if we keep a low profile. All we need to do is keep an eye on him every minute from now on. You guys should proceed as planned, taking Rudy over to Ida Cullerton's. Today. Now."

"What about you?" Frank asked.

"I told you," said Woody. "I'm scheduled for that chess tournament in Chicago."

"Well, too bad. That leaves it up to you, Doug,"

Frank said. "I have to practice the tuba. My lesson's tomorrow, you know."

Missy came running back, almost out of breath. "Doug, Mom says you and I have to go along with her."

"Go along where?"

"To see about renting things. A punch bowl and chairs . . . and things."

"Tell your mother he can't," Frank said. "It's up to Doug to take Rudy over to work."

I didn't care for the way Frank was making decisions for me. "Now, just a minute," I said. "My sister won't be put off unless she knows the reason why. And I'm not going to make up a story." I tried not to think of all the stories I'd told lately. "Besides, it's your turn to look after Rudy, Frank."

"Yeah, well what am I supposed to do about practicing?"

Woody put a hand on Frank's shoulder. "You can practice over at Ida Cullerton's, while Rudy's doing the lawn."

"What? Practice out there where everyone can see me?"

"It's the only way, Frank," Woody said. "It *is* your turn, you know."

Frank kicked at a clump of dirt, turned, and started walking away. "You'll have to bring Rudy over," he said to me over his shoulder. "You can't expect me to carry my tuba and my music stand and the sheet music and still lead that darned goat."

"Oh, all right." I turned to Missy. "How soon do we have to leave?"

"In about half an hour, Mother said. She's doing some sample painting on that fabric, just to satisfy Aunt Gloria. She'll put it out in the sun to dry while we're gone."

"Okay. Tell her I'll be there."

Woody and I decided the rope might be better than the heavy chain to tether Rudy while he was cropping the grass. We walked together toward Ida Cullerton's.

She was about to leave for her garden club meeting when we got to her yard. "I certainly do admire you boys for your ambition," she said, petting Rudy. "Your parents must be real proud of you. I just may call them later on and tell them how much I think of you."

"Oh . . . uh . . . you don't have to do that," I stammered.

"Now, don't be modest, dear," she said. "Well, I'll be getting along." She got into her car and drove away.

"Don't worry, Doug," Woody said, "most grownups just say things like that and then let it go. Well . . . I've got to run. Can you stay here until Frank shows up? I hope you can."

"Sure. If he makes it snappy."

Woody had just disappeared when Frank came into sight, lugging his big instrument and the music stand, which he hadn't bothered to fold up. The sheet music was rolled up and stuck in his hip pocket. "Where are you going to stake Rudy?" he asked.

To tell the truth, I hadn't even thought of bringing a stake, but I wasn't about to admit it. "Here's the rope," I said. "Fasten it wherever you want it. Around your neck for all I care."

Frank gave me a look of disgust. He stomped up to the front steps of the house, set down his music stand, put the music on it, picked it up when it fell, and put it back. Then he raised the tuba to his mouth. I'd heard him before, but from a distance. The blast was so strong, if I'd been wearing a wig it would have blown right off.

I glanced around. There was nothing to tether Rudy to except a tree in the corner of the yard. But from there he wouldn't be able to reach most of the grass. There was a post, though, on the front porch, next to the rose trellis. From there the rope would reach the main part of the yard. By then maybe Frank would be fed up with practicing, and hand-hold the rope while Rudy polished off the rest of the grass.

I tied Rudy to the post and backed off. Boy, if he ever needed earphones it was now, to block out those terrible sounds coming from the tuba. Should I run back to the clubhouse and get them? No, I didn't dare. If anyone spotted Rudy wearing that Walkman, it would be all over for us.

"'Bye for now, Rudy," I called. And like waitresses do in restaurants, I added, "Enjoy your meal." But I really didn't see how he could with Frank's tuba blaring in the background.

CHAPTER 12

Disaster Down the Street

SYLVIA WAS IN the back of the house putting the fabric on the bushes to dry. She'd painted big pink roses on it. "Where were you, Doug? I've been looking all over for you."

"Just down the street. Why?"

"What are all those bags and things down by the clubhouse?"

"Just stuff." It was lucky Rudy wasn't around. "Why were you looking for me?" I asked, trying to distract her.

"We're about ready to leave. As soon as Missy gets ready. Oh, here she is."

Our first stop was at the florist's. Missy seemed to enjoy the drawn-out discussion about wedding flowers, but I was edgy. Next we went to the rental place.

It was even more boring. Sylvia finally chose a punch bowl with cups, and arranged for folding chairs. "You absolutely promise to have everything there by ten A.M.?" Sylvia asked once more before we left.

"That wraps it up, doesn't it?" I said when we finally got going again. I was beginning to get nervous about leaving Frank over at Ida Cullerton's so long. You never knew about him.

"There are just a few more things I have to do," Sylvia said.

I was thinking there were a few things I had to do, too. First I had to go down and stash those plastic bags away somewhere. I'd totally forgotten about putting them at the curb on garbage pickup day.

But most of all, I had to get Rudy out of sight. Now that Sylvia had been down by the clubhouse once, she might go back again. If anyone had woman's intuition about something going on, it was my sister Sylvia.

We'd no more than pulled into our driveway when I flung out, saying, "I've got to talk to a friend of mine," and took off. Missy came hurtling behind me.

"I have this awful feeling something's going to go wrong," I said, breathing hard as we jogged along. "Like they're about to close in on us."

"I know," Missy said, huffing also. "I wish Woody would hurry and get home."

I didn't hear any tuba sounds from a distance, but Frank had probably finished practicing by now. When we came in sight of the yard, though, there was no sign of Frank, his tuba, or the music stand. There was also no sign of Rudy.

"What do you make of — oh no!" I stopped, too horrified to make another sound.

It wasn't just a case of something wrong. It was a case of total disaster!

"Oh no!" Missy gasped, coming to a dead stop beside me. "Oh no, I don't believe this!"

We had to believe it, though. It was all there, in front of us. The worst-looking mess I'd ever seen in my life!

As Missy and I stood there in a state of shock, Woody came breezing up on his bike. He braked, let out a low whistle, and said, "Frank just called and said the yard looks bad. He was wrong. It looks awful."

The grass in Ida's yard had been cropped down to the ground in some places. In other areas it stood up like spikes. Even that wasn't the worst of it. Where roses had twined in and out of the trellis, there were now only sickly-looking vines.

Missy made a little sound. "Imagine. All those leaves, roses, and thorns rumbling around in Rudy's tummy. The poor thing."

We were walking around, getting sicker by the minute, when Frank came chasing up. "Guys," he said, "it looks like we're really in for it."

"How in heck did all this happen?" I asked, really burned at Frank. "What did you do, go off and leave Rudy?"

"Hey, what kind of jerk do you think I am?" Before I could tell him he said, "I was here all the time. I just didn't happen to notice what Rudy was doing." He scowled. "So sue me."

"How could you happen not to notice?" Woody asked. "Where was your mind, Frank, while this was going on?"

"My mind was on my music, that's what. I had to practice out here in the open where everyone could see and hear me because you guys ducked out on me."

"Don't go putting the blame on us!" I yelled.

Woody shook his head as a warning for me not to get Frank more riled up. "Just sketch out the chain of events as they occurred, Frank. You were practicing, keeping one eye on Rudy, I presume?"

Frank twitched. "Sure, I kept an eye on him, what do you think? But after a while the sun got in my eyes and I had to turn away from Rudy or go blind."

"Oh, great!" I said. "You turned your back on our goat and didn't happen to notice he was gobbling everything in sight!"

"Just watch it, Doug, or I'll deck you!" Frank yelled.

"Not now," Woody advised. "In times of trouble club members stick together. And we're sure in trouble. Let's just hope Mrs. Cullerton, when she returns, doesn't call the cops."

"Someone already called," Frank said. "One of the neighbors."

Woody lost a little color. "Someone actually called the cops? About our goat?"

"Not about the goat," Frank said. "About my playing the tuba. They said I was creating a neighborhood nuisance. Disturbing the peace. What a lie. I was just going through my regular practice."

Woody was quite pale now, but his ears were turning a slow pink. "And what did the cops do when they got here?"

"They scared Rudy away with their sirens, that's what they did."

"Scared Rudy away!" I yelped. "Where is he now?"

Frank shrugged. "Your guess is as good as mine. He just took off down the street."

We all stared at Frank in shock.

"You let him get away?" Missy asked, eyes wide. "Without even going after him?"

"I couldn't, not with the police standing there. They'd think I was trying to make a break for it. I could have gotten shot!"

Missy tugged at my arm. "We've got to run and find him! Poor Rudy, he must be scared out of his mind!"

I was scared, myself. It was hard telling where or how far he'd gone. "You guys go down to the creek," I told Woody and Frank, "and then go off in opposite directions. Missy and I will check the street here and head toward my house." I struck my palm against my forehead. "Oh, man! Let's just hope Rudy didn't get into someone's garden. If he did, he's as good as goat stew right now!"

"Don't say that!" Missy shrieked. We all took off.

"Shall we go on?" Missy asked when we neared our house.

"Let's just take a minute to check the yard . . . and go down towards — "

At that moment Sylvia appeared in our driveway.

From the look on her face, I knew she knew. Missy and I stood still, staring at her.

Sylvia stared back. "So here you are," she said. "Out looking for someone?" She swept an arm in the direction of the bushes behind the house. We took a few steps and stopped.

There was Rudy. He was happy as could be, giving his famous goat grin. And from his mouth hung the last of Sylvia's flower-painted fabric.

CHAPTER 13

In a Whole Bunch of Trouble

FOR A MOMENT there was stunned silence. Then Missy moaned, "Rudy, how could you?" and reached out to take the last shred of cloth. She stretched it between her hands — a sad bit of what had once been fabric painted with pink roses.

"I see you know his name," Sylvia commented. "Whose goat is this, may I ask?"

Missy looked at me.

"It's Oliver's," I said. "A kid named Oliver."

"And how does Oliver's goat happen to be wandering around our yard?"

I shuffled. "It's a long story, Sylvia."

"Give me the condensed version."

"We're kind of watching the goat for Oliver. While he's gone."

"*Kind of*. What does that mean, exactly?"

I was hoping the telephone would ring or something. It didn't. I took a deep breath. "Oliver's on a trip, and so the guys and I are keeping Rudy for him. Down at the clubhouse."

"I see. And just how long have you been hiding this goat?"

I didn't like the "hiding" part. I shrugged. "A few days."

"And how long did you plan to keep him?"

I didn't like the "did you plan" part either. "We're keeping him until next Saturday."

"I'm not so sure you're . . . *Saturday*? Did you say *Saturday*? That's the day before the *wedding*!" she shrieked.

"Yeah. Well, Rudy will be gone. When the wedding is going on."

"Oh, wonderful, what a relief." The way Sylvia said that, I knew she was just being sarcastic. "You actually think I'm going to let that smelly creature roam around here until the day before — "

"He doesn't smell! And anyway, what if he did? How could it hurt anything to have a goat down at the clubhouse, minding his own business — "

"Like today. Why is he running loose today, may I ask?"

Oh, boy. In the heat of the moment I'd forgotten about the mess down at Ida Cullerton's. I needed time to think.

"That Frank was supposed to watch him," Missy piped up. "But . . ."

I could see that she'd remembered the Ida Cullerton scene, too, and didn't know how to go on. "But he didn't. Watch Rudy, I mean."

"This is all wonderful news, I must say." Sylvia suddenly looked weary instead of just angry. "With all the worry, with all the work I have to do, the last thing I need is more grief from you two. Or from a *goat*." She sighed. "Just look at that fabric I painted. Totally ruined."

"Mom," Missy said, "at least you know you're a good painter. Rudy must have thought those were real roses."

Sylvia just looked at her for a moment, and then she gave up. With a little laugh, she said, "All right. At least I have a good excuse now for not painting those gowns. As for the goat, get him out of here. Lock him up in the clubhouse until we decide what to do about him. It's out of my jurisdiction anyway. Dad will have to deal with this problem."

Missy and I took Rudy down by the clubhouse and sat around feeling miserable. Rudy didn't look as if he was feeling all that great himself. His problem seemed to be physical, though, not like the mental downer Missy and I were on.

"Do you think Grandpa will be furious when he finds out?" Missy asked.

"About our having Rudy here, or about Mrs. Cullerton's?"

"Both."

"I just don't know."

After a while Missy and I decided we might as well go up to the house. We tied Rudy to the stake, but we didn't put any food in the feeder, figuring he'd had enough for the day.

"Your friend Woody called," Sylvia said, taking vegetables out of the refrigerator. "I told him about the goat. About finding it here. He wondered why you hadn't called to let him know."

"Oh. I forgot." I swallowed. "Did he say anything else?"

"I didn't carry on a conversation with him. I just told him I knew everything and was very disappointed in all of you."

"You said 'everything'?"

"That's what I said." She got out the salad bowl.

Missy and I exchanged glances. I was wondering whether or not to take the plunge and really tell my sister everything when the phone rang. She picked it up.

It was Woody's mother, and I could tell pretty much what she was saying because my sister said, "Damage? What damage?" As the conversation continued, Sylvia's face showed surprise and then outrage. "You mean the entire yard? And the roses? But this is terrible!"

I started to shake. Boy, I was really in for it. Even Missy looked round-eyed and nervous.

"Oh, that poor, dear woman," Sylvia went on. "I had no idea this had happened. I do thank you for telling me. I'll have to talk to the children and to my father. And then I'll get back to you."

She hung up the phone and turned to us. "Well, Doug," she said. "This is a fine thing you've done." Her face looked like a tornado about to strike. "What have you to say for yourself?"

"Not guilty," I said without thinking.

"Not guilty!" The tornado picked up force. "How can you stand there and tell me you had nothing to do with this . . . this tearing up of poor Mrs. Cullerton's yard? How can you?"

Missy said softly, "But Doug was with us — shopping — when it happened."

"I don't need your input, Missy. And by the way, I do include you. You've been hanging around those boys and that miserable goat. You knew what was going on."

"She didn't have anything to do with it!" I didn't need to share the guilt with my niece. I had Frank and Woody to share it with. "It was just us guys — the club members. We made all the arrangements."

But Frank, I thought, was the real criminal. Him and his stupid tuba. "What about Frank's parents? What did they say?"

"Never mind about Frank's parents. The thing is, what will your father say?"

"Say about what?" Dad had just come into the kitchen. "What will I say about what?"

Sylvia stood there with arms folded. "Tell him, Doug."

I did. It sounded pretty bad. I mean, at first, over there at the yard, my biggest concern was for Rudy. But now I could tell I was in for it.

"I see," my father said when I'd finished. "Destroying property, disturbing the peace. Those are serious offenses."

I shook inside. Maybe I'd get hauled up before a judge. Thrown into solitary. Except Frank and Woody would be there, too. "We didn't mean for it to happen, Dad," I said.

"In a court of law, that's no excuse. It did happen. And you boys set up the conditions that made it happen."

Good old Missy went to bat for me once again. "Grandpa, it truly wasn't Doug's fault. It's that he trusted Frank. Aren't we supposed to trust people?" What a niece.

My father sighed. He looked tired. "I guess I'd better call Ida to assess the damage," he said to Sylvia. She nodded, gave us another storm-warning kind of look, and went back to preparing supper.

My father was on the phone for quite a while. I could tell Mrs. Cullerton wasn't being a mental case about it because my dad was saying things like, "Well, that's very nice, Ida, but the boys will have to fix things up." And, "No, I insist." Then he laughed a bit and said, "No, I won't do that. The punishment will fit the crime. I'll talk to the other boys' parents and get back to you later." Pause. "Well, that's really nice of you. Goodbye for now. And again, I really am sorry."

Missy and I had been setting the table while taking in the conversation. My father said, "Son, you're lucky Mrs. Cullerton is such a nice, even-tempered lady."

"She is very nice, Dad, and I'm sorry it had to happen to her. I wish there was something we could do about it."

"Oh, there is," My father said. I wasn't crazy about the way he said that or about the look that went with it. "We'll talk about it after we eat."

I really hate it when parents do that. Postpone talking until after the meal. I mean, how can you eat with knots in your stomach?

My sister Gloria breezed in just as we were sitting down to dinner. "Hi, family," she said. "What's going on?"

Everyone looked at everyone else. Finally Missy piped up. "Aunt Gloria, we've been keeping a goat for a friend. Down at the clubhouse. And he ate Mrs. Cullerton's roses."

"That's it in a nutshell," my father observed.

"A goat?" Gloria said helping herself to a roll. "Oh, then that must be the animal Scotty saw running around town."

"The goat?" my father asked.

"The goat?" Sylvia echoed.

"Well, sure," Gloria said, spreading on butter. "Scotty's wife was telling us about it at the beauty shop today. So it must have been the goat. What else could it be, running around town with earphones and all? I told them there was probably a logical explanation for it all, and now there is."

My dad and Sylvia looked at each other and then at me.

I shrugged. "We fastened a tape deck to Rudy because he loves country-western music. It was supposed to quiet him down."

My dad propped an elbow on the table and put a hand over his mouth. I could tell he was smiling but didn't want us to see it. Even Sylvia sat there shaking her head and trying not to smile.

Dad took away his hand. "But that doesn't account for the other incident — the face at the window, the ribbon, the round footprint. Or does it?"

"Grandpa," Missy said, "we made rainboots for Rudy so his fet wouldn't get wet. It's dangerous for a goat to get wet feet. And we tied them on with — "

"Pink ribbon!" Dad said. "Well, I'll be. Wait till I tell them about this down at the office."

"Dad, you didn't fire Scotty, did you?" I asked.

"No, I didn't, because it was obvious he hadn't been drinking. I didn't know *what* was going on, but I could see he was serious. And Doug, this is serious, too. Quite serious. You've been secretive and deceptive and destructive. We're going to have to discuss all this later."

That did it for my appetite. Missy's, too. There were lots of leftovers on this one day we didn't need them.

We took them down to Rudy anyway, partly to get out of the house and partly to make sure Rudy was chained. He sniffed politely at the food but I could tell he just couldn't handle any more, with those leaves and thorns and roses grinding away in his stomach. Prince polished everything off instead.

I scratched Rudy under the chin. "I don't care what they do to me," I said. "Just so they don't take you away ahead of time."

Missy looked alarmed. "Doug! Do you think they will?"

"I don't know," I said miserably. "I have the feeling Dad's talking to the other parents right now."

When Missy and I got back to the house, I found

that my mental radar had been right on target. The parents *had* been in conference.

"Well, son," Dad said, putting down the *National Geographic*, "we've decided on how you boys can make amends." He cleared his throat. "Between the three of you, you will have to mow Mrs. Cullerton's grass all summer. You'll have to keep the bushes trimmed, too. And you'll have to pay for the replacement of the rose bushes that were ruined."

Dad must have read my mind, because before I could say that I was flat broke he said we'd have to find jobs cutting grass for other people until we could raise the amount for new roses. "I'll advance the money, but you boys will have to pay it back." He smiled slightly. "I won't charge interest."

All in all it wasn't a bad punishment.

"How much longer is that animal going to be here, by the way?" Dad asked.

"Rudy? A few days is all. They'll get him Saturday."

"Good. Until then, you'd better make sure he doesn't cause any more problems. If he does, you'll have to get rid of him. I don't care where. To the animal shelter, if nowhere else."

"Oh, Grandpa!" Missy moaned. "Not the animal shelter! He'd die!"

My father couldn't bear to see his granddaughter distressed. He pulled Missy to him and gave her a hug. "You're not to worry about that goat," he said. "You just concentrate on being the best little junior brides-maid in the world."

Sylvia came into the room. "It's about bath- and bedtime for the best little junior bridesmaid," she said. "Did you ever show Grandpa your new shoes? No? Then run up and get them."

"They're divine, Grandpa," Missy said, running off.

"Divine," Sylvia said with a little laugh. "A Gloria word."

"Sylvia, don't you think you could let Missy have a pet?" Dad asked. "She really should have one. She has such a warm heart."

"Oh, Dad, not now. I have other things to worry about."

"I know. We really do appreciate it, your mother and I, the way you're helping out here. Don't do too much, though. This wedding is meant to be just a simple ceremony, for family and friends."

"I know, Dad. But I want it to be nice for Gloria. It's the only wedding she'll ever have. I hope."

Both Dad and I looked up when we heard the catch in her voice. I guess we were both thinking about Sylvia's marriage, and how it hadn't lasted.

Missy came back wearing the shoes. My dad said they were the most gorgeous he had ever seen. "And I've seen a lot," he added.

"Now off to bed," Sylvia said. "I'll come to tuck you in before I leave."

"Leave?" Missy stared at her mother. "Where are you going?"

"Oh, just out for a while."

"Out where?"

"To a new place, with music and dancing. Greg and Gloria are going, too."

"Why would you want to go dancing with Greg and Gloria?"

Sylvia gave a little forced laugh. "Well, Larry is coming along, too. So I won't be sitting there with just the lovebirds, if that's what's bothering you."

"That's not what's bothering me," Missy said, turning and walking up the stairs, chin held high.

There was a pause as Dad and Sylvia looked at each other.

"Is she always like this?" Dad asked. "Or is it just Larry?"

"I don't know." Sylvia looked toward the stairway. "Maybe I should just forget it. I don't *have* to go out."

"And you don't have to stay home, either," my father said. "Go. Have a good time. Relax. The child will get over it. She's probably just upset. It's been an eventful day."

"You said a mouthful, Dad," I commented.

I should have kept quiet. Both my dad and my sister turned to me and said, "Go to bed, Doug."

For once I didn't put up any objections.

CHAPTER 14

Maybe Mom Will
Marry Larry

MOM CALLED the next morning to say she'd be home soon — Thursday, in fact, so she didn't need to talk to everyone. I had started to leave for Mrs. Cullerton's but went back to get my cap. I heard Sylvia saying, "You wouldn't believe it, Mother. The kids have been keeping a goat down at the clubhouse." She paused, laughed, and said, "It surprised us, too. I'll save the details for when you get back." I was confused. Sylvia certainly hadn't thought our keeping the goat was funny before.

Missy had promised to keep an eye on Rudy in between final fittings for her dress. Frank and Woody met me over at Ida's. It was hard work. One of the hardest parts was to keep on going, because Mrs. Cullerton kept bringing out milk and cookies, and telling us not to overexert.

My dad drove up at around noon, bringing rosebushes for us to plant. When he saw the yard he shook his head. "It's incredible, this damage," he said. "You boys keep working until you get it fixed up," he said.

We shrugged at each other after Dad drove away. The yard *was* fixed up, as much as we could fix it, except for planting the roses. Mrs. Cullerton seemed pleased. "These roses are even nicer than the ones I had before," she said. "And as for the grass, it will grow back. We're just not going to worry about it."

When Woody and Frank and I finally finished, we took the yard equipment home and then had an emergency meeting at the clubhouse.

"Men," Woody said, "we've got to discuss finances. We're deep in debt. Not counting the outlay for the feed — which I was glad to cover for the time being — we have the companionship fee coming up, and — "

"Companionship fee?" Frank asked.

"The money we owe Oliver for letting us keep Rudy."

"That's a ripoff!" Frank shouted. "I told you so at the time!"

"You did not tell us so," I said. "You went along with it the same as Woody and I did."

"Let's not rake up the past," Woody said. "The issue is, how are we going to make money — fast?"

"I guess we can just kiss those other lawn jobs good-bye," Frank said.

Woody agreed. "Mrs. Cullerton's yard is not a good advertisement. However, it so happens I have thought of a new and better way to make big bucks. And this idea has nothing to do with grass or yards."

"Yeah? What's the idea?" I asked.

"Well, you know that people are supposed to remove

all the paper from their tin cans before they take them to the recycling center? But most people don't bother."

"So?"

"So that's where Rudy comes in. Goats don't really eat tin cans, of course, only the paper. They also like the taste of the glue. Well, my idea is to take Rudy over there to clean up the cans. For a fee, of course."

"Woody," I told him, "I hate to say this. But I can't believe people would pay a goat to do something they didn't intend to do in the first place. Face it, people don't care."

"I see what you mean." In a moment Woody snapped his fingers. "I know. We'll lay a guilt trip on them."

"Guilt trip?"

"Sure. Advertisements do it all the time. Make you feel guilty because you don't use their mouthwash or brew their brand of coffee. So we'll make people feel guilty about leaving those papers on their cans. Then we'll come up with the answer to their problem. I can see it now. A big sign that says:

NOW! SAVE TIME, SAVE ENERGY!
REMOVE LABELS BY GOAT POWER!
20 cans or less — 25¢

And then we can end up with some patriotic slogan like *Clean Cans for a Better America*! Hey, what's Rudy doing?"

He was gently butting me. "I guess he wants to play tag. Missy and I taught him how one day. You go up to him and say, 'Rudy, you're It!' And then he chases you and butts. Not hard. Want to see how it's done?"

"Doug," Woody said, "I will believe that only when I see it."

"All right." I went up to Rudy, told him he was It, and took off. Rudy came chasing behind me, and then slowed down to give me just a gentle butt. "Convinced?" I asked Woody.

"Not until I try." Woody went over, said, "Rudy, you're It," and started running. The same thing happened, only the butt Rudy gave Woody wasn't quite as gentle as the one he gave me.

"That is one smart creature," Woody remarked. "We'd be wasting his intelligence, hiring him out at the recycling center. Let's put that idea on hold and try to think of other ways to make use of his super goatbrain."

The grownups practically forgot about Rudy as the time grew nearer for the wedding.

"I'll pick up Mother at the train in the morning," Sylvia said to my dad one evening. "It'll give me a chance to catch her up on all of the details on the drive back. Oh — I keep forgetting to ask Gloria — will there be a wedding rehearsal, I wonder?"

"No," Missy piped up. "Aunt Gloria said we'd all go to the minister's Friday night, and he'll run through the ceremony. I get nervous just thinking about it."

"Sweetheart, you don't have to be nervous," my dad said. "Just stand up there and look beautiful. That's all you have to do."

"Wait until you see my dress!" Missy said. "Should I get it and show it to you now?"

"I'd rather wait and see the total picture," Dad said.

"I'm wearing a halo of flowers, did you know that?" Missy said. "So are the other bridesmaids, Alice and Tricia. And the new shoes, and the flowers — oh, I said flowers — and — "

"Missy, calm down," my sister said. "Have you finished eating?"

"Yes, I'm not hungry. I'll take the leftovers to Rudy."

Sylvia started to say something, but I guess she could tell by Missy's flushed face that she was too excited to clean off her plate.

Missy and I, along with Prince, went down to the clubhouse. It was a relief, at least, not to have to sneak around anymore.

While Rudy was enjoying the leftovers, Missy and I sat by the edge of the creek. We threw in pebbles now and then.

"I'll be glad when Mom gets here," I said, "but in a way it will make me sad, too. It'll mean that the time for Rudy to leave is getting closer."

"It's sad," Missy agreed. "Rudy will leave, and then after the wedding Greg and Gloria will leave, and then my mother and I will leave, too. I wish I could stay here the rest of the summer."

"Ask," I suggested.

"I already have. Mother said I couldn't. She said Grandma will be all worn out by then. I wish we'd move here."

"Hey, Missy, maybe you could! You know how?"

"How?"

"If your mom would marry that Larry guy."

"I don't think she would."

"Why not?"

"Well, she didn't that other time, when they went together. And besides, Mom wouldn't give up her career just for some guy."

"Couldn't she do her designing here?"

"I don't think so."

"I'll bet if you lived here you could have a dog."

"Yeah." Missy beamed. "A dog." She got up and tried to make a pebble skip but it didn't work. She stumbled and got her sneakers wet.

We heard Sylvia calling.

Making a face, Missy stomped water from her sneakers. "Yeah, Mom! Coming!" she yelled. And mumbled, "It's just to tell me she's leaving. With Lar-ry." She said it in a nasal way. "They're going to the movies."

"They ought to take us along," I said, as we went up to the house. "It's probably one of those PG pictures. I'd like to see one."

"Oh, sure, I can just see them taking us."

"Here you are, finally," was the way Sylvia greeted her daughter. "Say hello to Mr. Williams."

"Hello." Missy barely glanced at him. "We were down playing with Rudy. The old goat," she said, with a look at Larry.

"Now, why does a pretty little girl like you want to play with old dirty animals?" Larry asked. "Don't you have any dolls or nice teddy bears?"

Sylvia didn't give Missy a chance to say anything smart. "Look at you!" she said. "Hair a mess, shoes wet. Oh, Missy, what am I going to do with you?" She gave Larry one of those parent-to-parent looks that say, *Aren't children the limit? The things they do!*

Only instead of laughing and agreeing, old Larry frowned and said, "It seems to me that Missy lacks playmates of the right kind. Wouldn't you be better off playing with girls, dear?"

Missy scowled and said, "No, I don't think so. Anyway, there aren't any girls around here."

"Ah, but there are!" Larry looked as though he had something up his sleeve besides his arm. Sure enough, he went on, "As it happens, I have two little daughters about your age. I'll just bet the three of you could have some happy times together. Shall I bring them over someday soon?"

"How come you have custody?" Missy asked, still scowling.

Larry looked somewhat taken aback. "It's not a question of custody. The girls live just two blocks from me. I can see them whenever I wish. In fact, they're going to the movies with us tonight."

Sylvia's eyes blinked. "They are?"

"I was going to surprise you." Larry looked as though this was some big treat. "It happens that May — the girls' mother — is off on vacation. So I thought it would be a nice break for them to have a little outing tonight, away from the housekeeper. And it will be a good chance for you to get to know them."

Personally, I didn't think a movie was a great place to get to know someone, and I could tell my sister didn't think so either. But after a slight hesitation, she said, "That sounds lovely, Larry."

He actually beamed. As they were leaving he said, "And Missy, I'll bring the girls over to meet you soon. That's a promise."

"That's a promise," Missy mimicked as soon as they were out of earshot. "Oh boy, I can hardly wait." She folded her arms and jiggled them in an angry way. "You notice *we* don't get invited to go to the movies. Just the girls. His sweet, adorable girls. I'll bet they're real wimps."

"Why do you think that?"

"Because they're *his*."

"Come on, Missy." This kind of attitude wasn't going to help get Sylvia to marry the guy and move here. "How come you don't like Larry?"

"Who says I don't like Larry?"

"Well, do you?"

"No, I don't."

"How come?"

"Just because I don't."

I could see my niece was in one of her stubborn moods. When Missy gets that way, you might as well give up trying to hold a decent conversation.

I mumbled something about tucking Rudy in for the night, and went off. Missy didn't come after me.

When I finally got back, she was in the darkened living room, watching TV. From the reflected light I could see she had been crying. I sat down. Poor Missy. Her life must be pretty lonesome at times. Her mother gone a lot, and no dog.

We sat there quietly for a while, but then a quiz show

came on that had such weird contestants we just had to start laughing.

My dad came in and turned on a lamp, saying it wasn't good for the eyes, looking at TV in the dark.

I noticed the smudges on Missy's face, from crying. I guess Dad did, too. "You know, kids . . ." and then he said very seriously, "honk honk."

Missy smiled. She smiled even more when Dad went on, "I have an overwhelming urge for ice cream. Is there anyone in this room who would go along with me?"

"I will, Grandpa!" Missy squealed, and flung herself at him.

He kissed the side of her face and said, "Good. I was hoping for some support. You have three minutes to comb your hair."

Missy rushed upstairs. Boy, I have to admire my dad. He knew very well that when Missy looked into a mirror to comb she would notice the smudges and wipe them away.

"Can I go like this, Dad?"

"Sure," he said.

Missy rushed back. She looked fine. "I brought my notebook along," she said. "Are we going to the Thirty-one Flavors, Grandpa?"

He said yes. Missy always keeps track of what flavors they have, and how many. She said sometimes they don't actually have thirty-one.

CHAPTER 15

Missy Meets April and June

I DIDN'T GET to ride along when Sylvia, Missy, and Gloria drove to the train station in Chicago to bring Mom home. And why? To use my sister's exact words, "You can make yourself useful for a change, Doug, by cutting the grass."

It seemed only natural that I should offer to let Rudy do it. I'd stay right by him to see that he cropped the grass evenly, but oh no. "Don't bring that goat anywhere near the yard, Doug," Sylvia said. "It's bad enough to know he's down at the clubhouse. I don't want Mother to get upset about him. It'll be hard enough as it is, to keep her from getting nervous about the wedding."

Actually, when Mom stepped out of the car later, she didn't look a bit nervous to me. She came right over and gave me a big hug and kissed the top of my head. "Oh, lamb," she said, "I missed you so much."

"I missed you, too, Mom," I said. And I had.

"Grandma," Missy said, taking her hand, "do you want to go see Rudy?"

"Why, of course I do," Mom said. "Where is that famous goat?"

"Down at the clubhouse," I said. "Watch out, Mom, here comes Prince."

Prince leaped all over Mom until I gave him a shove. But she invited him to go along with us, not that he wouldn't have, anyway. "Just leave my bag on the porch," Mom said to Sylvia. "I'll be right back." Sylvia took it inside anyway.

"So this is Rudy," Mom said down by the stream, petting him on the head. "I understand you've had some wild adventures."

"I told Grandma about the rainboots and the Walkman and all," Missy said.

"Some boys down the street had a goat when I was a girl," Mother said. "I'll never forget that. Well, we'd better go up to the house and see what needs to be done. It's hard to believe the wedding's in just a couple of days."

Sylvia met us at the door. "Guess what. Uncle Jack just called to say he and Aunt Lorraine will be in tomorrow. Friday. 'To lend a hand,' was the way he put it."

Mom looked panicky at the news. "Where are we going to put them, Sylvia?"

"In a motel," my sister said firmly.

"Oh, we can't do that. Their feelings would be hurt,

especially when they're coming to help." Mom thought about it, then said, "I know. We'll put them in Doug's room."

"*What*?" I couldn't believe it. "My room! Then where am *I* supposed to sleep?"

"Oh, out on the porch. You've bunked out there before and liked it."

"Well, I don't like it now."

Around noon, my Aunt Gracie, who was on the outs with her husband, decided she'd come on Friday, too. I guess she was afraid she'd miss out on something. So she was to get Missy's room.

After that, Sylvia put her foot down. "Any more arrivals, early or not, go to the motel," she said. "Good heavens, there's enough going on around here without turning the place into a travel lodge."

Woody called. "You'll be happy to hear, Doug, that I've come up with a red-hot idea for making money. This one can't fail. There's no yard work involved." Woody cleared his throat. "When can we meet?"

"Come around this afternoon," I said. "I'll be here, working, as usual. I have to paint the trellis, Dad says."

"Trellis? What trellis?"

"In the backyard. The bride and groom are going to stand under it for the ceremony."

"It sounds beautiful. I'll bring lots of film for my camera."

"You're coming to the wedding?"

"Of course. All the neighbors are invited. Didn't you know?"

"How should I know? The only thing they tell me is what chore to do next. I'm just the unpaid help around here."

I was just about finished painting the trellis when Woody showed up. "You've done a fine job, Doug," he said, squinting against the sun. "You're a regular Michelangelo."

"Ha ha, make me laugh," I said. "My arm's about broken."

"Have you seen Frank?"

"Yeah." I walked around the trellis looking for any spots I'd missed. "He took Rudy for a walk. He'll be back any minute."

"Excellent. Is there anything else you have to do, or could we have a meeting?" He got his professor look. "I'm due to go out of office, as you must realize, and I — "

"There's another thing you must realize," I interrupted. "You're leaning on the trellis."

Woody snatched his hand away. He managed to rub most of the white paint off on the grass. "So can we have our meeting or not?"

"Sure. As soon as Frank gets back."

Woody walked with me to the garage while I put the paint stuff away. "It's been an exciting term for me in office," he went on. "Not always smooth, but certainly exciting. By the way, where's Missy?"

"In the house. I'll call her."

The three of us had just gotten to the clubhouse when Frank came along with Rudy. Old Prince carried on like a clown, he was so glad to see his pal.

"Everyone's nuts about this goat," Frank said. "I had kids following me like crazy. I sure wish I had a quarter for every kid who stopped to pet him."

Woody rubbed his hands together. "You must have read my mind, Frank. As you know, Sidewalk Days are almost upon us. . . ."

"Is that where the stores put stuff outside and sell it cheap?" Missy asked. "I love that."

Woody nodded. "Everyone loves a bargain," he said. "So the shoppers indeed enjoy it. And the merchants enjoy it, too, because it gives them a chance to unload stuff they'd be stuck with otherwise."

"All right, all right, everyone loves Sidewalk Days," Frank said. "Except us. Because we've got no money and nothing to sell, either."

"That's where you're wrong, Frank," Woody said. "Remember what you just said about everyone wanting to pet Rudy? Well, with my idea, people will get to pet him, and we'll get paid."

"Listen, I may be stupid," Frank said, "but you can't tell me that anyone is going to fork over money just so they can scratch a goat under the chin."

Woody smiled. "They won't pay directly. The merchant pays us to have Rudy on hand. Rudy will attract people. The people will then buy from the merchant. And everyone will be happy. See?"

None of us got it, but Missy was the one who admitted it.

Woody explained. "The merchant in question owns

a pet store. You know the one, guys — Harold's Hut?"

We said yes, we knew that shop. Every kid in town knew it.

"So. Harold naturally wants to attract people to his store. And what attracts people? Animals. But Harold doesn't want everyone handling his puppies and kittens and birds, and passing around germs, so he agrees to rent Rudy, for petting purposes."

Missy looked shocked. "He doesn't care what happens to the poor goat? Just because it's not his?"

"Oh come on," Frank said to Missy. "Rudy has a constitution of iron. A few little germs will be nothing to him."

"I have to agree with that," Woody said. "Not that I'm unfeeling, but Rudy does seem to enjoy a life free from most ills."

"Doug?" Missy appealed to me.

"I really think he'd enjoy it," I said. "You know how he loves attention."

"Tell me about it," Frank said. "I had to practically drag him away from the last three kids. He was like in goat heaven."

So we agreed to give it a shot. Sidewalk Days would start tomorrow, Friday, and continue through Saturday.

"It can only be Friday for Rudy, though," Frank said. "Too bad."

He meant *too bad* for losing out on money. Woody probably felt the same way, but at least he gave me a look of sympathy.

We heard Sylvia's voice calling, "Missy! Douglas!"

"I'll go see what she wants," Missy said. "Be right back."

While she was gone, Woody gave a long, drawn-out speech about how much it had meant to him to be president.

He was interrupted by Missy, calling from the top of the incline. "Doug!"

Woody asked for a motion that the meeting be adjourned. I made the motion and Frank seconded it as we hurried up the slope. "The meeting stands adjourned," Woody puffed out just as we reached the top.

Missy was standing there with two girls and Larry.

"Hi there, Doug," Larry said in a hearty way. "Nice seeing you again. I've brought my girls over to meet you and Missy."

"Oh." I motioned for Woody and Frank to come over.

"This is my daughter June, and this is April," Larry said.

"Hiya. This is Woody . . . and Frank."

Everyone mumbled a greeting while giving each other the once over.

Larry, acting like some quiz show host, said, "I thought you kids might want to get to know each other, before the wedding."

"Wedding!" the taller girl yelped. "Who's getting married?"

"June, don't you remember Daddy telling you? Missy's aunt Gloria is getting married. I thought you remembered."

"You thought wrong."

If I'd have made a smart answer like that to my father, I'd have been in for it, but Larry just looked embarrassed.

June went on, "Are you saying we're invited to her aunt's wedding?"

"We sure are," her father said. "All of us."

"Even Mother?" April asked.

June gave her sister a jab with her elbow. Then, eyeing her father, she said, "It would be a bit awkward, wouldn't it? For Mother to be here, with father's girlfriend around?"

"June!" Larry gave her a dirty look. "April, stop that inane giggling!" He was probably sorry he had started all this. "I'll leave you all to get acquainted," he said.

We just stood there, watching him leave. Then Woody came to the rescue. "So," he said, smiling at the girls. "It's April and June, is it? Whatever happened to May?"

"Nothing has happened to Mommy," April said. "She's just on vacation."

She got another jab from June. The poor kid had to have a chronic case of black and blue marks along her ribs. "April," her sister said, "you don't need to answer when someone is just trying to be funny."

April grinned and hunched her shoulders up and down.

"I'm not trying to be funny," Woody said, his ears turning pink again. "I'm just trying to make conversation."

"Well, don't try so hard," June said.

Woody just wouldn't give up. Turning back to April, he said, "On what day in April is your birthday?"

April gave a big skinny grin and hunched her shoulders up and down again. She seemed to have two expressions: A small grin and a big grin. She said, "My birthday is in November."

"Interesting." Woody asked June, "And when is your birthday?"

"In June, naturally."

"Oh." Woody blinked. "Naturally."

June, I later realized, also had two expressions. Hers were *suspicious* and *hostile*. She gave Woody the hostile number. "My mother is May, because she was born in May. I am June because I was born in June. So what do you expect — she'd name my sister *November*? How stupid can you get?"

At that point Prince came frisking up, thinking probably that a party was going on. Rudy, left alone down by the creek, started bleating.

"That's our goat," Missy said to June. "Want to see him?"

"All right."

We all scrambled down the incline. Rudy trotted up, friendly as could be. June shrank back. "Get that animal . . . get *it* away from me!"

I caught Rudy by the head just as he was about to butt her. "Don't ever say that word" — I spelled *i-t* — "around Rudy. We say that when we play tag with him. Want to see?" I walked a little bit away then turned and said, "Rudy, you're *It*!" He took off after me and gave me a gentle butt. "See?" I said to the girls. "So be careful and say it only when you want to play tag."

June glared at Rudy. "I don't want to have to be careful of every little thing I say. Can't you get rid of the dumb goat? Put him in that shed over there."

For once, Woody forgot his manners. "Listen, lady," he said, spitting out little specks. "That's not a shed, that's our clubhouse."

Putting up a hand, June backed away in disgust. "Just say it, don't spray it!"

It again!

Missy caught Rudy just as he was about to take off. I had the feeling he wanted to butt June on general principles. Goats can tell when they're not liked. They have feelings.

"Let's go up to the house," Missy said. "Prince, stay here with Rudy." He did. Woody and Frank said they'd keep the animals company. They weren't so dumb. I'd rather have stayed at the clubhouse, too, but I was pretty sure Missy would need someone to side with her against those creepy girls.

The girls' father was in the kitchen, having iced tea with my mom and Sylvia. "Back so soon?" he asked. "Did you kids hit it off okay?"

No one answered.

"How about a cold drink?" Sylvia asked, starting to rise.

"No thanks," June said. "Dad, we have to leave."

Larry, looking embarrassed, got up saying he and the girls had things to do, and he knew Mom and Sylvia were busy also. My sister walked out with them. Missy and I stayed in the kitchen with Mom.

"What happened?" Sylvia asked when she came back in.

"Happened? Nothing," I said.

"Nothing," Missy echoed.

Sylvia didn't seem to know what to make of it. She was too busy, though, to give us the old third degree. "I'm going to run upstairs," she said to Mom, "to see if there are fresh towels in the bathroom."

In the silence after Sylvia left I glanced up to see my mother looking at Missy. I looked, too.

My niece was sitting there at the table with a worried expression. She was chewing on the ends of her hair, a nervous habit I thought she'd stopped a couple of years ago.

"Missy . . ." Mom said. "Come sit on Grandma's lap." Missy's legs looked odd, dangling down from Mom's lap, but I didn't smile or even stare. It didn't matter how big Missy was. She just needed to be held and hugged at that moment.

My sister started to come back in, but when she saw Mom cuddling and comforting Missy, she stopped. She looked startled and then almost teary as she turned and left again.

It was peaceful there for those few minutes. After all the cleaning and cooking and phone calls, we needed this little time out. I could remember such moments with Mom when I was a little kid. Times when I was hurt or scared or tired, or just needed to be comforted.

I almost wished that just for a while I could be little again. I was sad, too, but in a different way from Missy.

It was a kind of sadness most people wouldn't under-stand. I could just hear them say, "You're feeling down because of a *goat*? Such nonsense!"

It was important to me, though. I loved Rudy and he loved me. But soon we'd be separated. There wasn't even a place in the house where I could let go and maybe even cry about losing Rudy. Wherever I went, there would be too many people around.

The only place where I could be alone that weekend was the clubhouse. I didn't know, though, if I could ever have fun there again. There'd be too many re-minders of Rudy.

CHAPTER 16

Good-bye, Rudy

THOSE LAST TWO days before the wedding flew by like a speeded-up movie film.

I tried to stay clear of the house. Everyone was acting hyper, as though the whole world was set to watch the wedding on prime time.

The relatives who arrived early, as they said they would, really got in the way. They kept asking what they could do, but no one had time to explain where anything was or what to do with it. Poor Missy got stuck with the relatives the most because she was in the wedding party and knew most of the stuff they wanted to hear about.

I did what any kid would do if he had the chance. I got out of there. Down at the clubhouse Frank was about to leave with Rudy. "I'll stay with him this morning for Sidewalk Day, and you guys can do it this afternoon," he said.

"Fine," Woody agreed. "In the meantime, Doug, we might start to clean out this clubhouse." He walked to the door of it. "Get rid of this carpet, and put these bags of used shells out on the curb. We should have been putting them out all along."

We rolled up the pieces of carpet and stuck them in garbage bags. Then we dragged them up to the front of the house. We were just hauling up the last of the bags with peanut shells, the ones that smelled so bad, when Sylvia came outside.

"What's in those bags?" she asked.

"Just stuff from Rudy," I told her. And then, to make her feel good, I added, "We wanted the place to be nice for the wedding."

I thought she'd be pleased, but instead a shocked look came over her face. "You intend to leave that smelly stuff out front? Garbage pickup isn't until next Wednesday!"

"So? Is there any harm in cleaning up ahead of time?"

"There most certainly is!" She still looked fairly shocked. "Do you think we want those bags on display, for our guests? You boys just pick them up and trot them back down there out of sight."

We did.

Missy gave the relatives the slip and walked along to the pet store in the afternoon with Woody and me.

"I wish Rudy could stay," Missy said. "I'd be willing to send half of my allowance every week to help take care of him."

Woody looked at her curiously. "Why would you do that, Missy?"

"Just because Doug loves him so much."

"Wow," Woody said. "Doug, you have one super niece."

I couldn't trust myself to speak. All I could do was nod my head.

We could see several kids clustered around Rudy in front of the pet store. Before we quite got up to him, Rudy raised his head, sniffed, and bolted toward us. He butted against me in that gentle way of his and raised his head to be scratched under the chin.

"Sure can tell you're the boy who owns this goat," Harold of Harold's Hut said.

I didn't tell Harold he was wrong. To Rudy, I murmured, "Don't worry. I'll stick around, boy. Now let these kids pet you."

He had fresh water, I saw, and still some of the feed Frank had brought along for him. There was a constant stream of kids, out for Sidewalk Day with their parents or just looking for bargains on their own. They lined up, waiting their turn to pet Rudy and talk to him.

Woody and Missy took off after a while to hunt for good buys themselves. None of the sale stuff interested me. I wanted to be with Rudy and make the most of the short time we had together.

By five o'clock most of the people had gone, and taken their children with them. Missy and Woody came back. Missy had found a terry cloth toaster cover with *Hot Stuff* printed on it for Gloria. Woody had saved a lot of money on batteries for the various gadgets he owned.

Harold forked over ten dollars and said he sure wished Rudy could come back the next day.

On the walk home Rudy stayed close to me, as though he sensed we'd soon be parted. I kept putting out my hand to touch his head. I hoped he'd understand, when the time came, that his being taken away wasn't my idea. I really wished there was some way to let him know that.

We had a buffet-style dinner that night because, with some of the relatives there, plus friends of Gloria that dropped by, there wasn't enough room for a regular sit-down meal.

Afterward, Missy and the rest of the wedding party went to the minister's to go over what everyone would say or do at the ceremony.

Taking Prince along, I went down to the clubhouse to keep Rudy company. Rudy gave me his little sideways look, so I played tag with him for a while. I wondered if he'd enjoy it as much if he knew this was to be our last time together. I counted the hours. Twelve, maybe, before Oliver and his dad came to get Rudy. I couldn't waste one of those hours.

Telling Rudy I'd be right back, I went up to the house and got my sleeping bag and flashlight. I wrote a note to Missy to tell her where I'd be, in case someone was looking for me, and put it on her cot. As an afterthought, I got an old quilt for Rudy to lie on. As another afterthought, I took a box of cookies from the cupboard. Mom wouldn't care.

When I put down the quilt outside the clubhouse Rudy went right over and stretched out on it. He was really one smart goat. I put my sleeping bag beside him and sat there telling him things I'd never told anyone. After a long time I stretched out and fell asleep. Once, during the night, I woke up, and the minute I stirred Rudy nuzzled me. It was as though he was keeping watch over me.

Missy shook me awake at dawn. "You'd better come up to the house before the others wake up," she said. "No one missed you."

"Has Oliver called? About when they'll be here?"

"No."

He still hadn't called by ten-thirty, when Woody and Frank showed up. "Maybe they decided to hang out camping for another day," Frank said. "Or maybe their car broke down."

Right then, without any warning, the truck pulled into the driveway. Frank and Woody went over to Oliver and asked about the trip. I stayed close to Rudy, fighting the urge to take hold of his chain and run.

Woody walked back to me and said in a lowered tone, "I floated a loan from a source I have, so let me handle the finances. We can figure out who owes what later."

It was all right by me. How could I think of money at a time like this?

"Hey, boy," Oliver's dad yelled, "would you stop that jawing and get over and help put up the ramps? I got more things to do today than fool around with this darned goat!"

They set the ramps, and then Oliver dragged Rudy by the chain and got him into the back of the truck. Rudy began bellowing like crazy.

Oliver and his dad and Woody got into a conversation. At one point the father turned and shouted, "Rudy, shut up, will you, or I'll come up there and shut you up once and for all!"

Rudy began bleating piteously. I couldn't even calm him down when I went around to the back of the truck. He looked so sad I thought my heart would break.

Suddenly Prince bolted outside through the screen door and began tearing around and barking up a storm. He knew something was wrong. Then he must have decided Oliver's dad was the mean guy. Old Prince bared his fangs and crept along the ground with a low growl. He sure looked ready to spring.

"Get that blasted hound away from me!" Oliver's dad yelled. "What's the matter with him, anyway?"

I grabbed Prince by the collar and managed to hold him, but it wasn't easy.

Rudy began bellowing again. "Shut up, I said!" the man yelled. "Come on, Oliver, get in the truck." He was shoving money into his pocket. "I see where I'm going to have to beat that goat back into shape!"

By this time, my dad, my mom, my aunt Gracie, my aunt Lorraine and my uncle Jack were all coming outside.

Just as my dad stepped toward the truck, it started with a lurch that hurled Rudy against the side. "Hey!"

my dad yelled. But the truck took off, with Rudy bleating in a way that went right through me.

I heard Missy cry out and other voices saying things like, "What's going on?" and "Oh, that poor creature," and someone calling my name.

With tears spurting, I ran down to the clubhouse. The guys followed after.

"Hey, Doug, Rudy will be all right," Woody said. "Oliver's father just talks tough. That's his way. He wouldn't hurt Rudy."

I didn't answer. I just sat there, my knees drawn up and my head down, crying for all I was worth. I didn't care if the guys did see me. Crying was the only thing I could do.

"We'll leave you alone," Woody said. "I know you don't want to hear about it right now, but I managed to get a better deal, moneywise."

I didn't answer.

Woody touched my shoulder. "We'll talk later. Come on, Frank." I heard them go away.

After a while, when I stopped sobbing, I still sat there with my head on my knees. I felt someone near me. Missy. Or maybe Mom.

Then a voice said, "I know it's tough, Doug. It really is tough."

I raised my head. Sylvia!

Without thinking, I twisted and leaned against her. She put her arms around me as I began to sob again.

Finally, when I was all cried out, she brushed my hair back and wiped tear streaks away with the palm of her hand.

"Want to go up to the house now?" she asked with concern.

"Might as well."

Whatever had been said about the goat was finished when I walked into the house. The grownups were careful to talk about other things and not notice how I looked. Rudy wasn't mentioned even once.

Somehow the day went on.

CHAPTER 17

An Uninvited Wedding Guest

T HE SUN SHINING into the screened-in porch
woke me up the next morning. Sunday . . . Gloria's
wedding day at last. I wrapped my pillow around my
head, but it was no use. I was wide-awake.

"Aren't we lucky?" Missy said, from her rollaway cot.
"A beautiful day, just the kind we hoped to have."

"Yeah. Well, I'm glad for Gloria's sake. For everyone's."

Mom had said she just couldn't bring herself to think
of what would happen if it rained. We had relatives
hanging from the rafters as it was. And then if we had
to crowd all the neighbors and friends who were
primed for the occasion into our house . . . well.

Just then Sylvia came out to the porch. "I thought I
heard voices," she said. "I'm glad you two are awake.
How about getting up and dressed so we can clear
away this bedding?"

"Oh, Mommy, I'm so excited! And nervous!" Missy said. "I hope I don't goof up during the ceremony."

Sylvia gave her a hug. "You won't, sugar."

"When will the flowers get here?" Missy asked as I was gathering up my clothes. I didn't have to get all dressed up until later.

"Just before noon," Sylvia said. "Missy, get into your jeans and top quickly while no one's around." I was leaving by then.

When I came back into the kitchen, Sylvia was there, putting out cereal, fruit, and milk. "You guys eat fast before the mob descends," she said. "I'm going back up to Gloria, who's having an attack of nerves."

After she was gone, Missy told me what the wedding ceremony would be like. "We all walk up to the trellis, and Greg and Gloria stand under it, facing the minister. The best man stands next to Greg, and Tricia and Alice stand next to Gloria, and me next to them."

"How long is the ceremony going to take, anyway?" I asked. "I hope it's short and sweet."

"I think it will be. The minister will say a few words first. I guess something about them hanging together even if they get sick of each other. Then Greg and Gloria put rings on each other's fingers. They just pretended at the rehearsal."

"Is that it?"

"No. The minister says, 'I now pronounce you man and wife.' Then . . . here comes the part you'll hate. The minister says to Greg, 'You may kiss the bride.' They practiced that. A lot."

"That's pretty sickening. Will they really kiss at the wedding, right in front of everyone? I can't believe Greg would do it."

"I think he will," Missy said. "He didn't seem to mind."

"Well. Let's change the subject. I *am* trying to eat breakfast, you know."

"Doug, you're really mean. I hope you won't do anything or say anything to spoil the wedding. People are supposed to be happy at times like this."

"I'll be happy, all right. When the stupid thing is all over. And everyone leaves. And I can get my room back."

An angry look came over Missy's face, but just as suddenly it dissolved. In a quiet voice, she said, "I know you're feeling sad. I don't blame you. I felt sad when they took Rudy away, but I know it's worse for you. A lot worse."

"I'll get over it," I said, my voice cracking a little. "I'd rather not talk about it just now, though."

Someone called in from the porch. "Anybody here need a wedding cake?"

Missy ran to let Mrs. Langley in. "Where's the cake?" I heard her ask.

"It's out in the station wagon. I just want to be sure the table's ready."

Sylvia and Mom came downstairs. They went into the dining room where the white cloth and candles and stuff were all set up. Then some man — Mr. Langley, I guess — and some young woman and Mrs. Langley herself started bringing in the cake, layer by layer.

Missy and I stood over to the side while they put the thing together. There was a layer, then some pillars, then another layer, more pillars, and finally the top layer. The whole thing was swoshed over with pink and green and white icing. Mrs. Langley had a squeeze gadget that she used to make even more frosting flowers, now that the cake was all assembled. On the very top were bride and groom dolls that almost ruined it, in my opinion.

By the time Mrs. Langley had squeezed out the last bit of icing, my mom, my dad, Aunt Lorraine and Uncle Jack, and Aunt Gracie were all buzzing around. Then in came Gloria. She didn't have on a speck of makeup, but she didn't need any. She had a glow about her. Mom put her arms around Gloria and kissed her, and Aunt Gracie went into a crying fit, saying, "Oh, I hope it works out for her, but you just never know!" Aunt Lorraine told Aunt Gracie to cut that out.

The rest of the morning was like a TV set when you keep hitting the remote-control button to change channels. People were eating, laughing, talking, getting ready, all at the same time. The phone never stopped ringing. My dad just sat by it in the kitchen, halfway reading the Sunday paper between calls.

The tagalong relatives who were staying in motels showed up. The flowers arrived, someone brought in sacks of ice for the champagne, and the bridesmaids arrived, sounding like a pair of hyenas.

Mom called me. "Doug," she said, "could you do something with Prince? He's driving everyone crazy."

I knew if I put him in the clubhouse he'd howl and

really drive everyone bananas. I took him over to Woody's instead.

"No problem," Woody said. "I'll put him in the garage. Look, I've even got some leftovers. It'll seem strange not to save them for Rudy anymore. That goat certainly scarfed up the food."

I didn't want to talk about Rudy. "I'd better get back," I said, looking at my new wristwatch. Twelve-thirty already!

"Where'd you get that?" Woody reached for my wrist. "Neat. Does it do anything? Besides tell time?"

"It plays 'Yankee Doodle Dandy.' Gloria and Greg gave it to me. They said I was a junior best man in spirit if not in fact. They gave Missy a watch, too."

"Listen," Woody said, "do you want to shower while you're here? It must be bumper to bumper traffic in front of your upstairs bathroom."

"Mom made me shower last night. But I've still got to go and get dressed. So long. See you later."

I could hardly get through the kitchen, it was so packed with people. My aunts had taken over so the family could get dressed. I passed Sylvia on my way upstairs. "Doug!" she said. "Aren't you ready yet? Scoot! The guests are arriving." She was wearing a peach-colored dress, and she had her hair pulled to one side, with flowers in it. She would have looked like a knockout if she hadn't had that worried expression.

I got the "Aren't you dressed yet?" routine from Mom, too, upstairs. She had a worried look to match my sister's. "Hurry up," she said. "And then go down and help your uncles seat the guests outside, on those folding chairs."

I hadn't heard anything about there being music, but when I came back out, five guys were over to one side of the yard, playing slurpy love songs. People were beginning to settle in the chairs. My uncle Jack told me to try to round up the strays and get them seated. "But don't seat anyone up front there, where you see the white ribbons. Those are reserved for the family."

In a while everyone settled down. The piece the guys played then must have meant something because everyone stopped talking. The relatives came out, and then Mom and Sylvia. Someone pushed me forward, and I ended up in the front row, next to Mom. Greg and his best man walked down the porch steps and then stood to one side of the trellis. Was I ever glad I wasn't up there!

There was a short silence, and after that the musicians played "Here Comes the Bride." Even I knew that one.

Tricia and Alice came out, looking pretty good, and Missy followed them. Her dress was pink, like the grownup bridesmaids', and she was carrying a nosegay. All three of them had wreaths of flowers on their heads, too. I could hear people whisper, "Isn't she adorable?" when they saw Missy. I glanced over at Sylvia. Her eyes were moist.

Then the audience made an "ohhhh" sound and I could see why. My sister Gloria walked down the steps looking — I have to say this — like an angel. She was so pretty it brought a lump to your throat. Greg seemed about ready to pass out.

My dad, who had brought Gloria out, moved back, and Greg stepped forward to the trellis beside Gloria. Dad came and sat on the other side of Mom and took her hand. She looked kind of teary-eyed, too.

I could see why the minister didn't say his speech at the rehearsal. Who'd ever want to go through that boring stuff twice? While he went on and on about how great marriage was, I began looking around for Woody and Frank. I couldn't see them, but I did see Larry and his wimpy kids. April was grinning and June was looking hostile, as usual.

Just as I was checking those girls out, I saw their eyes widen and their mouths drop open. Everyone else's eyes seemed to widen and their mouths dropped open, too. I swiveled around to see what it was that had caused those looks, and I nearly fell off my chair.

Wandering up the lawn, and looking mighty pleased to be there, was no one else but Rudy!

"Good heavens!" I heard my father say. My mother, frozen, was clutching Dad's arm like crazy. Sylvia looked like someone in a horror movie who'd just caught sight of the chain-saw killer. I just felt numb.

The audience was buzzing a bit, but not enough to make the bridal party notice. The minister kept reading out of his book, and Greg and Gloria were off in a world of their own. Missy, though, out of the corner of her eye, had caught sight of Rudy, who was now happily coming toward her. And what did Missy do?

That kid is so great. Without turning around, she put her hands behind her, still holding the nosegay of flowers. Rudy sniffed them with great interest and nibbled at a rose.

I couldn't have moved if I had to.

Some people in the crowd began buzzing a little louder, and there was light laughter, but others shushed them. Rudy was really into the bridal lunch by now, and enjoying it a lot. He had just polished off the last white rose when the minister said to Gloria and Greg, "I now pronounce you . . ."

At that very moment, Rudy raised his head and went, "*Maaaaa . . .*"

"Maaah . . . man . . . and wife," the minister said. Then he caught sight of Rudy. "Where did that goat come from?" he gasped.

"May he kiss the bride?" Gloria prompted, her eyes only on Greg.

"No, he may not!" the minister shouted. "The idea!"

The audience roared.

Flushing, the minister turned back to the bridal pair. "Yes, yes, by all means, Greg, kiss the bride!"

Everyone was laughing now, except the bride and groom, who were kissing as though it was going out of style.

"Get that blasted goat out of there," Sylvia said to me, teeth clenched.

I bent down, hoping that would put me out of sight, and went up to Rudy. He turned and nuzzled my neck.

"Come on, Rudy," I whispered. "The party's over. For you." I took him by the collar, pulled him off to one side, and led him down the slope. He frisked around happily, sticking close while I found the rope in the clubhouse and fastened it to his collar and then to the stake. "How did you get here, anyway?" I murmured. "You sure stole the show, Rudy."

Woody and Frank came scooting down the incline. "How did he get here?" was what they wanted to know, too. It wasn't until later that we found out Rudy had jumped the fence at Oliver's and managed to find his way back to our house.

I gave Rudy a good scratching under his chin and a promise of cake, and then went back to the wedding.

It was all over, and everyone was kissing anything that moved and saying it was the most beautiful wedding they could remember. There were a few remarks about Rudy, but not as many as you'd expect. Even Sylvia was so busy being the hostess that all she said to me was, "Tell people the newlyweds are going to cut the cake inside the house now."

Woody, who was taking about as many pictures as the official photographer, got on the hall stairs for overhead shots of the big cake-cutting ceremony in the dining room. Gloria cut a few slices, and then one of the aunts took over. Not everyone could squeeze inside the house, so they were passing along plates of cake to people in the yard.

"Hey, Missy," Woody yelled down into the crush of people. She looked up, and he took her picture. Then she wiggled through and got to us on the stairs.

"You were real cool," Woody told her. "Holding those flowers behind you to distract Rudy."

"I didn't even stop to think," she said. "I just did it."

"Uh-oh," Frank said. "Get moving. Here come those creepy *month* girls."

April and June were trying to move toward us, but they were hemmed in. We spotted an opening and made it outside. Then Gloria and Greg appeared on the porch steps.

"She's going to throw the bridal bouquet!" someone shouted.

Woody got his camera in focus. He took a shot of Gloria with the bouquet held aloft, and then he quickly turned the camera toward the bridesmaids, Tricia and Alice. They were jumping up and down and squealing, "Me! Here, Gloria!"

Gloria pitched the bouquet in their direction, but both girls missed. The flowers fell to the ground, the girls bent down at the same time, cracked heads with a loud thump, and sprawled on the grass. It was a moment I'll always remember, and my pal Woody got it on film.

After a while we went back inside to see if the second piece of cake would taste as good as the first. It did. So did the third and fourth. There was still a lot left over.

Remembering my promise to Rudy, I filled a paper plate with broken pieces of cake and odds and ends of icing some of the dieters had left behind. I sneaked off a couple of extra roses, too.

Rudy gave me a little nudge of thanks and went to it. He seemed to like the icing flowers even better than the real ones in Missy's bouquet. For an extra dessert after his cake, he ate the paper plate.

"Rudy," I told him, "I'll bet this is one wedding everyone will always remember."

Rudy looked at me with his famous goat grin. And then he gave a delicate little belch. I guess that was his own way of saying he was happy to have been a part of it.

CHAPTER 18

The Wicked Step-Sisters Take Off

I WASN'T IN a big hurry to get back to the wedding scene, but on the other hand I didn't want to miss out on anything.

About half of the people were still in the yard, sitting around on chairs, visiting, or else standing in little groups.

Gloria, Greg, the bridesmaids, and their friends were still whooping it up. Mom and Sylvia were being the hostesses, mingling among the guests, seeing that they were all having a good time. They didn't seem to notice me.

Dad did, though. He, too, was with a group, but he was giving me the old evil eye. I drifted over to where Missy and the guys and Larry's wimpy daughters were hanging around when Dad appeared and put a hand on my shoulder.

"Hi, Dad," I said, looking up with my most friendly kind of expression. "Seems like a nice party."

He didn't return the friendly look. "Have you noti-fied your friend about that goat showing up here?"

"Oliver?"

"If that's his name. Have you?"

"Not yet."

"And why not?"

"I . . . uh . . . didn't want to tie up the telephone."

"I see. Well, go tie it up. Now."

"What should I say to Oliver?"

"How should I know what you should say? What *do* you say in a case like this?"

"You want them to come get Rudy now? Right away?"

"The sooner the — " He stopped, looked around at the guests, and said, "This evening. Tell them to come this evening. And in the meantime I don't want to see that goat, hear that goat, or be reminded of that goat in any other way. Go make the call."

I did. It was my bad luck that Oliver's dad answered the phone. I told him not to worry about Rudy, he was here and okay.

"That lousy animal!" he shouted. "He's been bellow-ing night and day and kicking up a ruckus and now he's run off! Wait till I get my hands on him!"

I began trembling. "Rudy was pretty good when he was here."

"Yeah, well maybe that's the problem. He had it too good. You've gone and ruined that goat, that's what you've done. It's going to take a while to lick him back into shape!"

My stomach churned. "Would you want to leave him

here for a day or two?" I hoped the man might cool down by that time. I'd explain to Dad. He'd see that it was necessary.

"Leave him there to get even more rotten spoiled? Not on your life. I'm going to come get him and beat the tar out of him!"

"No, you can't!" My stomach gave another lurch. "We've got company. You can't come here before evening. My dad says!"

"I'll be there." He hung up.

Just before I put down the receiver I thought I heard a little gasp. *Oh no, Missy*, I thought. *I hope you weren't listening in.* I felt too miserable to go see, though. "Beat the tar out of him," Oliver's dad had said. He didn't mean it. He couldn't. People didn't beat animals. But maybe Oliver's dad was different. And he certainly did sound angry enough. Maybe he'd cool down in a little while. I had to believe that. I sat there breathing in and out, to quiet my feeling of nausea.

After a while I went downstairs. Outside, I saw that most of the guests had gone. One of the neighbors asked me if that was my goat that had wandered in. I told him, no, it belonged to a guy I know.

"Ask him if he has any goat fertilizer he wants to sell," the man said. "It's great for gardens."

I just nodded and looked around for the kids. They weren't in sight, so I headed for the clubhouse. Sure enough, Missy, Frank, and Woody were there, watching Prince and Rudy frisk around as though they hadn't a care in the world. To my annoyance I saw April and June were there as well.

"Where have you been?" Woody asked.

"Dad made me call and tell Oliver's dad that Rudy is here."

"What did he say?"

Because Missy was listening, I said, "Just that they'll come to pick him up this evening." Then, to get off that subject, I told Woody about the neighbor who wanted to buy goat fertilizer.

Woody slapped his palm against his forehead. "How could I have overlooked that idea?" Then he brightened. "But we still have all those bags full of the stuff over there. They should bring a nice bit of change. Lucky we didn't leave them out for the pickup after all."

June made a face. "Goat fertilizer! That is the most disgusting thing I have ever heard of!" She turned to Missy. "How can you stand to be around boys like this and not get sick or something?" Without waiting for a reply, she called over to her sister, "Come on, April. We're leaving. Daddy wouldn't want us to be here."

April, standing by the creek, said, "Just a minute, June. I saw a little fish just now."

"Oh, you did not," June said irritably. "We're leaving right now. Come on!"

"I did too see a fish," April yelled, "and if you say I didn't, you're just a dumb old kid."

June looked furious at being put down by her sister, but she tried to rise above it. Lifting her chin, she said, "A kid is really a goat, you know. So if there's a dumb kid around here, Rudy is it!"

It struck all of us at once, but we were too stunned

to move. Not Rudy. He'd heard those words, *Rudy is it*, and with lowered head he started for June.

"Oh no!" Missy yelled. "Rudy!"

It was too late. Rudy was charging, and with a shriek June took off. Right away she made a mistake. Instead of heading up the hill, she tore down toward the creek. Seeing her error, she stopped, just at the edge of the stream. Rudy didn't stop. He gave her a butt from behind and sent her flopping full length into the muddy water.

It happened so fast that everyone froze for a moment. But then we ran toward the girls. June, by this time, had gotten back on her feet and stood in the creek, a dripping, muddy mess. She didn't stand there long, though. With a wail like a fire engine, she tore up the slope, her once-white shoes oozing mud at every step. April, though untouched, ran off screaming, too.

We stood there looking at each other in pure horror. Missy started shaking. I wasn't feeling too steady myself.

"Well . . . uh . . . that was an unexpected turn of events," Woody finally said. "In a day marked by unusual events."

"What'll they do to you?" Frank asked, giving a nod toward the house.

"I don't know," I said. "I just don't know."

"Hey, it wasn't your fault," Woody said. "Didn't we warn that June creature not to say 'it' around Rudy? Is it your fault if she didn't listen?"

"No, but somehow it's going to turn out my fault anyway. Just wait."

Missy was still shaking. "Oh, Doug, they may ground you or something, but it will be over with and done. In my case . . ." She put her fists up to her mouth.

"Hey, Missy, they're not going to blame you," I said.

"I know that. It's worse. What if . . ." her eyes were round and frightened. "What if my mother and their father . . ." She bit her lip. "They'd be my *step-sisters*!"

That gave us something to think about all right.

"Wicked step-sisters," Missy went on. "Like in 'Cinderella.' Only there won't be any prince. . . ."

At the sound of his name Prince leaped around, barking for attention again and acting like a real nut.

"I'll take him back," Woody said. "The last thing you need right now is a hyper dog."

"Yeah, I'll help you take him home," Frank said, glancing up toward the house.

Missy and I looked at each other. We had to face them sometime. It was better to go up ourselves than to have them come fetch us.

It was around sunset now, and the yard was deserted except for Sylvia and Larry and his two girls, all standing in the driveway. Sylvia was wrapping a big towel around June and saying, "Well, Larry, I really *am* sorry!"

"*Sorry* hardly does it, do you think?" Wow, he looked mad. "As though it wasn't bad enough that the beast made a shambles of the ceremony . . ."

"Oh, come on, Larry. The goat didn't ruin the wedding. As a matter of fact, I thought he added a touch of fun."

Missy and I were standing a little way off, taking all this in. But the grownups were so into arguing that they didn't notice us.

"Fun, you say!" Larry yelled back. "I must say you have a strange idea of fun." And then, "So maybe it's not so strange that you've got a couple of young savages running around here who —"

"Hey, just a minute! You're talking about my kid and my kid brother!"

"—who need to be taught a few things!"

"I'll worry about that!" Sylvia snapped back.

"Come, girls," Larry said. "Get into the car. Now, stop crying, both of you. Daddy isn't mad at *you!*"

"I'll take care of the cleaning bill," Sylvia said. "And Larry, I'm really sorry, though I won't agree it was all Missy and Doug's fault, not until I hear the whole story."

Larry looked grim. He got into the car, said, "I'll return the towel," and left without even saying good-bye.

As Sylvia turned to go into the house, we walked over to join her. "You heard all that?" she asked.

"Yeah." I shook my head. "He sure was mad."

"You know, I'd forgotten that about him," Sylvia said. "His temper. And his total lack of humor."

"I guess he didn't think what happened to June was funny," I said.

"That about says it," she agreed. We walked toward the back porch, but then she sat down on the steps and we sat beside her. She draped an arm around each of us and said, "Suppose you give me the scoop about what really happened. I can't believe you'd sic that goat on June, Missy." She paused. "*Can* you sic a goat?"

"That's what she claimed?" I was really furious. "Sylvia, Missy didn't do a thing!" And then I told her what really happened.

Sylvia shook her head. "It's so far-fetched it must be true," she said. "Nothing about this wedding was what you'd call ordinary." She gave a little laugh. "When I saw that goat strolling up toward the trellis, pleased as could be . . ."

Missy, still looking anxious, said, "Did it ruin the wedding for Aunt Gloria and Uncle Greg, do you think?"

"Oh, honey." Sylvia gave each of us a squeeze. "Those two were in dreamland all day. They probably won't believe the wedding took place until they see the pictures." She gave a tiny sigh. "It must be nice to be in a rosy cloud. To love so much . . ."

Missy snuggled closer to her mother. "I'm sorry you and Larry had to fight," she said. But in a small little voice she added, "I hope you don't make up."

Sylvia kissed the top of Missy's head. "I'm sorry it ended this way," she said. "But then again, maybe I'm not. It's over. No regrets." She scrambled to her feet. "Hey, guys, here we are out yakking, and there's stuff to be done. Let's go in and see what we can do to help."

CHAPTER 19

And They Lived Happily Ever After

M Y PARENTS WERE in the living room with the relatives, who were just getting ready to leave.

"Oh, there you are," Aunt Lorraine said. "We were just wondering what happened to the three of you."

"Just tying up loose ends," Sylvia said. "Do you really all have to leave? So soon?"

We said goodbye all around. As the grownups came back from the cars, Mom told Missy and me to go upstairs and change clothes. She said we were going out to dinner, but no place fancy.

"I can't go," I told her.

"Oh? Why not?"

"Because they're coming to get Rudy. This evening. I've got to be here." My voice cracked a little.

"I see." Mom touched my shoulder. "Go up and change anyway. Then you'll be ready. We'll all wait with you until . . . until after they've been here."

Missy and I went upstairs. My body felt like lead. I got out any old thing and put it on. What did I care how I looked when I was falling apart?

Missy called into the room, "See you downstairs."

Suddenly she came back. "Doug," she whispered, "They're talking downstairs. Mom and Grandma and Grandpa."

"So?"

"About us." She paused. "And about Rudy. I'll go wait for you on the stairway."

When I came out she motioned for me to be quiet. Sylvia was talking.

". . . didn't mean to listen in," she was saying, "but something in Doug's voice really got to me. He was terrified, and I could see why. That man . . . that man who owns the goat . . . sounded horrible. He actually said he was going to whip that goat into shape."

"Oh, surely that was just talk," my father said.

"I don't think so, Dad. I really believe he meant it."

"Sylvia, there are laws against mistreating animals."

"Yes, and there are people who ignore those laws."

It was quiet then, and Missy and I started down. Then the grownups began talking again. We stopped.

Dad said something I couldn't quite catch and then, "But I just can't see keeping a goat on the premises."

"Oh, Dad. Remember when Gloria and I had the rabbits? And that whole string of cats? You said it was good training for kids — being responsible for pets. And we did take care of them. Just as Doug would look after that goat."

"He does seem awfully fond of it, Clarence," my mother piped in. "I've never known him to care that much about any animal."

"What about Prince?"

"Oh, hon," my mother said, "it's not the same. That dog will lick any hand that feeds him. The goat, though, seems to have a real attachment for Doug. I've never seen anything like it."

My dad still wasn't giving in. "Sylvia, if you're so concerned about your young brother, what about your daughter? I don't see her with any creatures, big, small, or otherwise."

"I've been thinking about that," Sylvia said. "I really have."

"All right. I'll give some thought to the goat," Dad said. "Right now, though, I'm going to go upstairs and change into something more comfortable. They put too much starch in this shirt collar."

"Yes, let's all get ready," Mom said.

My niece and I raced up the stairs, and then turned and were starting down as they were coming up. "Oh, hi," Missy said. "We're ready to go."

Dad squeezed her waist as he went by. "We'll be with you in a minute, J.B." He winked. "Junior Bridesmaid."

Down in the dining room we saw empty, sticky punch cups everywhere, and plates with cake remains. The rest of the cake, almost the whole bottom layer, was still there with icing roses just ready to be picked off. I was thinking of taking another helping down to Rudy when I heard a truck in the driveway, doors slamming, and then Oliver's dad shouting, "All right, go get that animal!"

Missy ran out. For a moment I couldn't move. Then I started to go out, but turned and headed up the stairs to get Dad. Missy hurried back inside, screaming, "Doug! Oh, Doug! He's got a whip! He's going to whip Rudy!" She went screaming upstairs.

I ran outside just in time to see Oliver come up the slope, yanking on Rudy's chain, and the father advancing toward Rudy with the whip.

"Don't you dare hit him!" I yelled.

Mr. Newhart turned to me in a rage. "Just shut your mouth, kid. This is no business of yours!"

"It *is* my business!"

The ramp was in place, but Rudy, bleating, refused to go up it. The man struck out with the whip.

Running to shield Rudy, I slid on the gravel of the driveway and sprawled. By the time I got up, the ramps were gone, and Rudy was in the truck, bellowing like crazy.

"Stop!" I yelled. "Don't you dare drive away!" But Oliver and his dad were already in the truck. They zapped out of the driveway as my dad and Missy came out, Dad in just his undershirt and pants.

"Hey!" Dad yelled. The truck kept on going.

Dad lit out for the garage. "Come on, kids," he yelled, "get in!"

We took out after the truck. It barely made it through a yellow light. We had to stop for a red.

"Oh, Grandpa, they're way ahead now," Missy

sobbed. "I'm afraid Rudy's going to fall and break a leg — look how fast they're going!"

A police car pulled up next to us.

Dad called out of his window, "Mike, stop that truck up ahead!"

The police car zoomed on, red lights flashing and siren going. It made the truck pull over. We stopped just behind and got out of the car.

Rudy was almost howling in anguish. Oliver sat in the truck cab, wide-eyed, his nose pressed against the glass. His dad was out talking to the cop.

"Exceeding the speed limit," the policeman was saying. He raised an eyebrow at Dad.

"Plus cruelty to animals," Dad said.

Missy and I left the men to argue. We went over to the back of the truck where Rudy was now shivering and making pitiful little bleating sounds.

"Don't worry, fella," I said, reaching up to touch his leg. "We're going to take care of you." But were we? What could we do?

The men were still talking, only now Oliver's dad was a lot quieter.

Then they all separated.

"Come on, kids, get back in the car," Dad said to us. He looked grim.

The police car, the truck, and our car all turned and headed back toward our house. Missy and I kept looking at Dad, but no one said anything. I was almost afraid to breathe.

We pulled into our driveway next to the truck. The

police car stayed out at the curb.

Without a word, Oliver's dad got out the ramps again, and reached up toward Rudy. Rudy backed away, bleating.

I went forward. "Come on, Rudy. It's all right, boy."

He came to me, and I led him down the ramp.

"Take him, Doug," my dad said. "He's yours."

I started shaking all over.

Oliver, who was standing there watching, said "Yeah, Good riddance. I was sick of taking care of that goat anyway."

"I'll send you a check tomorrow," Dad said to Oliver's father.

"No rush, no rush at all. Take your time. I'll bring over some feed and things."

"Never mind," Dad said. "We'll handle it."

They threw the ramps up into the bed of the truck and took off again. Once they were gone, the police car pulled away.

Mom and Sylvia were outside by this time.

"Well, Doug," Mom said, a hand on my shoulder. "It looks as though you've got your goat, son."

I had such a lump in my throat I could only shake my head. Tears were streaming down my face. I didn't care.

"Oh, Doug," Missy crooned. "I'm so happy for you — and Rudy!"

As big as she was, my dad picked her up. "Be happy for yourself, too, sweetheart. You're going to get your dog. Isn't that right, Sylvia?"

Sylvia shook her head and smiled. "What can I say? Yes, Missy, you're going to get a dog. What a day. What a wedding. What a family."

We were all so happy and so keyed up we decided not to go out to eat after all.

"Let's just scramble some eggs or have pancakes or something else simple," my mother said. "It doesn't matter what we eat. We'll just enjoy being here together."

At that moment Prince dashed up, giving excited little barks. "Well, Prince, come on in the house," Mom said. "We don't want your nose to get out of joint just because we have a new pet in the family." Prince didn't need to be told twice.

Missy and I were still outside, stroking and soothing Rudy, when Woody came puffing up. "Prince got out of the house and headed this way, and so — " He stopped. "Haven't they come to get Rudy yet?"

"Been here and gone," I said. "But Rudy stays."

For once, Woody was absolutely speechless.

"It's like a fairy tale," Missy said dreamily. "The wicked stepsisters are gone, the mean man is punished by the police, and the goat goes to the boy who loves him most."

"And what about the fairy princess?" Woody asked. "What happens to her?"

Missy smiled. "She gets the dog."

"The dog?" Woody looked around. "What dog? Prince?"

"No. His name will be Wishbone. He's what I've

wished for, time after time. And now it's come true."

"No kidding."

"No kidding, honk honk. Wishbone's for real."

He was, too. Missy brought him along the next time she and Sylvia came to visit. Rudy loved Wishbone right away. Wishbone loved Rudy.

As for Prince . . . he just went on loving everybody.